AT
YOUR
SERVICE

Heartbreak Cafe #3

Janet Quin-Harkin

FAWCETT GIRLS ONLY · NEW YORK

RLI: $\dfrac{\text{VL 6 \& up}}{\text{IL 7 \& up}}$

A Fawcett Girls Only Book
Published by Ballantine Books
Copyright © 1990 by Daniel Weiss Associates, Inc. and Janet
Quin-Harkin

Library of Congress Catalog Card Number: 89-91912

ISBN 0-449-14532-8

Manufactured in the United States of America

First Edition: March 1990

Chapter 1 _____

*I*f anyone had asked me which one of my friends would suddenly go bananas, I would never in a million years have picked Pam. Pam has been my best friend since kindergarten, when she brought a new lunch box (Sesame Street, I think it was—or maybe the Flintstones) and I had no snack with me and she gave me half her sandwich and a cookie. Since then I have relied on Pam for more than sandwiches. I rely on her to share the good times and also to keep me from rushing off and doing crazy things; I rely on her to be there when I need to talk. Sometimes I think Pam was born wise. She was even sane back in junior high, when we were all stupid and giggly. She didn't want us to toilet-paper houses or ring doorbells or spy on the guys' locker room. She always had her homework done and was never caught daydreaming in class. She never did anything reckless or wild in her whole life until I persuaded her to come with me to the Heart-break Cafe last summer. I don't know, maybe it

1

wasn't my fault; but the Heartbreak's definitely where the trouble began.

We had only been out of school for a week when I decided that life this summer could end up pretty boring. Outside of working at the café, I did not have any big plans—or anyone to plan big things with. Since my parents' divorce, my mother and I had moved out of our house and were now living at The Oaks, a "planned community for today's living," which in reality was a dreary condo project. I guess there might have been some kids my age living there, but I was still too overwhelmed by culture shock and too much of a snob to want to meet them. For me the condo was merely a place to sleep, and I didn't want to make it any more than that.

Any other summer I would have had Pam around, lounging by the pool at my place or going for long walks near her house, or even making cookies together since Pam loved to eat. We had always done everything together. But after helping me get over my parents' divorce, Pam was going through a crisis of her own: her grandmother had come to live with her family a few weeks earlier, just until they could get her a place at a nursing home. Pam had not talked much about it at first, but now that school was out, the strain was really beginning to show. I really found out that something was wrong for the first time when she showed up at the Heartbreak a few days after school was out.

Things had been kind of chaotic all morning because my boss, Mr. Garbarini, had another doctor's appointment, and he was always in a bad mood when he had to go back to his doctor. He had had a heart attack earlier in the year and was still supposed to be taking it easy, but he was a stubborn old man, and the only way you'd get him to stand still was to nail his feet to the floor. He was arguing nonstop in the kitchen with his grandson, Joe, who was my other boss (and who was also beginning to play a larger and larger part in my life, but more on that later). I was running around them, trying to broil burgers, fill glasses, and get orders out to the tables, so I barely had time to stop when I saw Pam come in.

"Hi, stranger," I called to her as I whisked past with three skillfully balanced plates in my arms. "Haven't seen you in ages. Things are real crazy around here today!"

Just then, Mr. Garbarini's loud voice boomed from the kitchen: "I told you before, I don't need a doctor. I'm perfectly healthy!"

"Then maybe I'd better not stay," she said hesitantly. But I saw something in her eyes as they met mine—a kind of hopelessness that I had never seen there before. "I guess you haven't got time to talk."

"Hang on a minute," I said. "Let me get these orders out and maybe things will quiet down. Okay?"

"I could come back another time," she said. "It's just that I keep calling your house and you're never home."

"Things always quiet down by midafternoon," I said. "Don't go, Pam, really. I'll bring you a chocolate madness," I offered. Then I remembered that the people at the next table were waiting impatiently for their food.

"Bribery will get you everywhere," she said, managing a smile. "I'll wait."

At that moment Joe and his grandfather appeared. The old man was still growling. "Doctors! Who needs doctors! All they want is my money. They're a waste of time, always saying the same thing: 'Rest, Mr. Garbarini. Eat healthy, Mr. Garbarini!' And what do they mean by eat healthy? They mean rabbit food, that's what they mean!" he shouted. A few months ago, an attack like this one would have terrified me, but now I was used to it. I'd learned to get used to a lot of things since coming to work at the Heartbreak.

"Quit griping and get going," Joe said, flashing me an exasperated grin as he shoved his grandfather toward the door. "They'll only get mad if you're late."

"I can walk! I can walk!" the old man insisted. "I'm not in my grave yet."

"You will be soon if you don't listen to the doctor," Joe said calmly.

"Pah, doctors," the old man muttered. "Who needs them? Nothing wrong with me that a good glass of red wine won't cure!"

"What a terrible old man," Pam whispered to me. "He makes my grandmother look meek and mild."

"He's not really so scary," I said. "He's just mad about being sick."

"I can drive myself," Mr. Garbarini was complaining as Joe opened the front door. "I'm not a cripple, am I?"

Joe shot me a despairing glance as he ushered his grandfather through the door ahead of him. "I think we're in for a real fun afternoon again," he said. "Can you handle things alone for a while?"

"Don't worry, I'll manage," I said.

He gave me a beaming smile. "Thanks," he said. "I'll make it up to you sometime." His words were so full of hidden meaning that I actually blushed. Pam was quick to notice.

"He'll make it up to you sometime?" she asked, raising an eyebrow, which she could do as well as Mr. Spock. "And you keep telling me there's nothing going on between you and Joe."

"There isn't," I said quickly. "He just meant he'd let me work a shorter shift one evening."

"Oh, sure," she said, grinning.

"So there was nothing to the rumor that a certain guy drove a certain girl home very late one night, and that she wasn't too heartbroken about breaking up with her boyfriend only a few days later?"

"You sound like a gossip columnist," I said. "I've told you a zillion times—Joe is just my boss. He's still dating the famous Wendy, and even if he weren't, I wouldn't be interested."

"I see," she said.

"You don't believe me?"

"I saw the way he looked at you," Pam said thoughtfully. "I wish just once in my life a boy would look at me like that."

"He was just squinting because the sun was in

his eyes," I said. "Now let me serve that table in the corner and then I'll get your chocolate madness." I ran off before Pam could say anything else. Even though she was my best friend, I found it hard to talk to her about me and Joe. Maybe that was because I didn't know what to think about him myself. One minute we were fighting, and the next minute we were pals. I finished the chocolate madness, putting on an extra scoop of whipped cream and a double helping of nuts, and carried it out to her.

"Here," I said. "How does this look?"

"Fine. Thanks," she said, picking up a spoon and poking idly at the whipped cream instead of attacking it as usual. "I just hope this will do the trick."

"I guess you're really upset about your grandmother, huh," I said.

She nodded. "It's so hard," she said. "I couldn't stand being at home a second longer, Debbie. I had to get out."

"Is she very sick?" I asked. We had no relatives living nearby and I'd had no experience with old or sick people, so I didn't really know what to say. Pam's answer surprised me.

"She was being difficult about food again."

"The caviar wasn't flown in direct from Russia, or was it that the coffee wasn't mountain grown?" I quipped, not quite understanding what she was getting at.

She made a face and looked embarrassed. "No, Grandma was throwing it around a lot," she said.

"She does that these days. I just missed getting a plate of spaghetti in my face."

"Oh," I said, feeling suddenly lame. I'd never suspected that Pam's grandmother was anything more than old and sick—a frail old thing who had to be looked after.

She shrugged her shoulders and gave an embarrassed grin. "She has Alzheimer's disease. It's not her fault that she's started acting crazy. Let's not talk about her, okay?" Pam said. "I came out to be cheered up. I am going to eat this sinfully delicious dessert that my best friend created for me and talk about happy things." She took a big spoonful, going through all the layers—the chocolate brownie on the bottom, the chocolate ice cream above it, then the chocolate syrup, the whipped cream, and the nuts—and gave a sigh of contentment. "We should go into business for ourselves and just make these things," she said. "We'd make a fortune."

"No way." I laughed. "We'd eat the profits."

Pam laughed, too. "Maybe you're right," she said. "I don't know how you can serve chocolate madnesses to other people all day. I'd have to take a scoop of every one I made!"

"Now that you mention it, it does look pretty tempting," I said.

"Here, take some," she said, handing me the spoon. "I shouldn't eat it all anyway, although I don't have the heart to diet seriously with all this tension at home."

I took the spoon and scooped a little ice cream that had slipped off the top.

"Go ahead, take more than that," she insisted.

"Every calorie you eat is one that won't wind up on my thighs." She looked up and sighed. "I just wish that Ashley had been right, that you could break things in half and let the calories escape."

We both laughed and looked over at the table where Ashley usually sat. She was our resident airhead—obsessed with dating and dieting. Ashley was always coming up with the most amazing theories on how to lose weight.

"Where is she, anyway?" Pam asked. "I don't recognize anybody in here today."

"It's because of this good weather," I said. "Nobody leaves the beach until the sun goes down. Ashley's working on a serious tan. She's trying to outtan Wendy so that Joe will notice her."

Pam shook her head. "She never gives up, does she? Do you think she'll ever realize she's not Joe's type?"

"Probably not." I grinned. "It's hard, though, when Joe's type is nearly anything that wears a skirt and doesn't play bagpipes."

"And yet he's stuck with Wendy all this time," Pam commented. "Amazing. I guess he must be getting tired of her and looking around for someone new?" She raised her eyebrow again as she asked the question. I pretended I didn't get her meaning.

"I don't think he's getting tired of her," I said. "He talks to her on the phone at least a dozen times a day, and he's always trying to sneak out early because Wendy wants to see a movie. She's even started picking out his clothes."

"I guess she must be pretty special," Pam said. "What does she look like? Gorgeous?"

I shrugged. "I haven't seen her close up," I said. "I've seen her in the car when she comes to pick up Joe, and I've seen her picture, of course. She looks like the total Miss Popular Cheerleader. You know, lots of blond hair, about a zillion perfect teeth, and big wide eyes, just like the girls in the Miss Tropical Suntan contest."

Pam grinned, more to herself than me. "You wouldn't be just a tad jealous, would you?"

"Me? Jealous? Don't be dumb," I said. "Why should I be jealous of her?"

"No reason, I guess," she said. "So, you've never met Wendy face-to-face?"

"No," I said. "She's never actually been in the café. I think Joe keeps her away deliberately. You know how the gang around here is—they're terrible teases. He probably doesn't want to put her through that."

"How sweet," Pam said thoughtfully. "Did you ever consider that maybe he wants to keep her away from you?"

"No," I said quickly. "I never even thought of that. There's no reason for him to keep her away from me."

Pam shrugged. "She just might not understand, you know. You and Joe together all the time, kidding around, teasing each other. She might get the wrong impression. She might suspect that under all that teasing you really like each other."

"Will you stop going on about Joe and me?" I

snapped. "Or I'll never make you another chocolate madness as long as I live."

"Now that is a serious threat," Pam said. "In fact,
that is one of the best deterrents I've ever heard.
Debbie? What's the matter? You look as if you've
seen a ghost."

I was staring past her, toward the front door. A
girl had just come in and was standing in the doorway, looking around with an annoyed pout on her
pretty pink lips. Her gaze swept the entire café
once more, then she tossed back her mane of
strawberry blond curls. She was even more beautiful than she was in her pictures.

"Speak of the devil," I whispered to Pam. "I think
you're about to meet the famous Wendy!"

Chapter 2 ⎯⎯⎯⎯⎯⎯⎯⎯⎯⎯⎯⎯

*T*he girl continued to stand there, as though she expected servants to flock to her side. I almost expected it myself. It was suddenly clear to me why Joe, who had never in his life kept a girlfriend for more than a month, came running to the phone whenever she called. And as I looked at her a thought crept into my mind before I could stop it: I could never compete with someone like that. As long as she was around, I wouldn't stand a chance with Joe! Then I scolded myself for thinking such a thing. I didn't want to stand a chance with Joe.

"Are you sure that's her?" Pam whispered.

"Pretty sure," I whispered back. "But there's only one way to find out." I walked over to her.

"Hi, can I help you?" I asked.

Slowly those big, blue eyes focused on me. The look in them made it clear their owner thought I was the lowest form of life. Her shrewd gaze traveled from my head to my toes, then she managed a weak little smile.

"I don't think so, thank you. I'm just looking for Joe—you know, Joe Garbarini. He runs this place."

"I know Joe," I said, and I think I put more stress on *know* than I meant to because I swear I saw her long eyelashes quiver. "I work for him," I added.

"Really?" she asked.

"You must be Wendy," I said.

She beamed, but still managed to look superior. "Right! How did you guess?"

"I've seen a picture of you," I said. "Joe showed it to me."

"Really? How sweet. He shows *everyone* pictures of me. Isn't that sweet of him?"

I didn't like the way she stressed the word *everyone*, as if I were just one of the teeming millions around Joe.

"I'm Debbie, by the way," I said. "I guess he's mentioned me."

She paused, then shook her head so that earrings jangled. "No," she said, "I don't think so. We don't talk about his work much when we're together. Where is he, anyway?" she asked.

"He's not here," I said. I was very tempted to leave it at that, but politeness won out. "He had to take his grandfather to the doctor's," I said.

The pout returned. "Oh, rats," she said, "and I stopped by specially."

"He'll be back later," I said. "You're welcome to wait. I could get you a soda or something."

She wrinkled her nose. "No, thanks," she said. "I have to stay on my diet if I want to fit into my cheerleading outfit at camp this summer. And I have to get my hair cut at three. I'll call him this evening. Just tell him I stopped by, okay?"

"Okay," I said.

"Thanks," she said with a tight smile. "What was your name again?"

"Debbie," I said.

"Debbie," she repeated so she'd remember it. "Well, nice meeting you. I guess you'll be seeing me again sometime, now that summer's here. Are you the regular waitress here?"

"That's me," I said. "The regular waitress."

"Great," she said, sounding super friendly. "Well, I'd better let you get back to work or Joe will be mad at us both, right?"

"Right," I said. "I have to get the floors scrubbed and the chimney swept before he comes back."

Either the sarcasm was lost on her or she wasn't really listening, because she just nodded and turned to the door. "You will tell Joe I came by?"

"How could I forget?" I asked.

"Well, bye then. I've got to fly," she said, and left.

I turned back to Pam, caught her eyes, and burst out laughing.

"I bet he doesn't like her for her brains," she muttered to me as I came back to her table.

"No, but there's not much wrong with her looks," I said, sliding into the seat opposite her. "She really is gorgeous, isn't she? And I don't think she's as dumb as she makes out, either. She got some digs in there—did you hear?"

"Every word," Pam said. "It was very entertaining. Two lionesses fighting over one lion."

I felt my cheeks flushing. "I was not fighting," I said. "I was just trying to do my job and act pleasantly to a customer."

"Oh, sure," Pam said with a grin. "If looks could kill, you'd both be sprawled on the floor by now."

"Don't be stupid," I said. Letting out a long sigh, I added, "What do I have to do to convince you that I would never want to date him? We are total, complete opposites. We disagree on everything that matters. He is the world's worst chauvinist, he's intolerant, ignorant, bigoted—"

"And very sexy," Pam added.

I had to laugh. "Okay, I guess he is sexy—to some girls," I said.

"To *most* girls," Pam said. "To all girls who don't have defective vision. Those muscles . . . those incredible brown curls . . . those gorgeous eyes . . . wow!"

"I'm surprised at you, Pam Paulson," I said. "I would have thought you'd be more interested in the intellectual type."

"No way," she said.

"I go for the sophisticated type myself," I put in.

"Like Grant?" Pam asked. "I thought you said he was boring."

"He was," I admitted, and sighed.

"I bet Joe's not boring," Pam said.

Remembering the couple of occasions when I had wound up in Joe's arms—by accident, of course—I had to agree I certainly had not found him boring then. I pushed the memories firmly from my mind.

"And speaking of not boring . . ." Pam was saying. I realized her gaze had drifted past me and out the window. A bright red sports car had pulled up outside the Heartbreak. The car had painted flames shooting down its side, oversized wheels, and a stereo blaring loud rock. A boy was getting out of it. He looked even more untamed than Joe, dressed in a big black leather jacket and very tight black jeans, which were torn at one knee. His dark hair fell to his shoulders. He was the sort of boy I would avoid if he passed me in the hall at school. Slamming the car door, he began to walk toward the café.

"Wow," Pam whispered.

The café door came flying open. He stood in the doorway and looked around, just the way Wendy had. His look of superiority pretty much mirrored hers, too, only he didn't pout.

"Any of you guys know where there's a good auto-repair shop near here?" he asked. His voice was deep and husky, as if he had been shouting at a long football game. "My friend's car's about to die on me, and I got to get it fixed or he'll kill me."

The café was almost empty. Usually some of Joe's friends who knew about cars would be hanging around, but today there were only a few customers, most of them girls.

"There's Brady's, just off Main Street," I volunteered.

"Do they know anything?" he demanded. "This isn't an ordinary car, you know."

"Ask for Terry," I said. "He races cars, so I'm sure he knows what he's doing."

The guy looked around, obviously trying to decide what to do.

"What's the problem?" Pam asked suddenly.

The guy looked as surprised as I felt. "I think it's about to boil over," he said. "I'm no grease monkey, but I think the radiator's shot."

"It could just be the thermostat," Pam said. "They should try that first. It would only cost you a couple of dollars to replace it."

"No kidding?" he asked. "You know about cars?"

Pam blushed. "My d-dad owns a . . . a service station," she stammered as he turned his full attention to her.

"No kidding?" he asked again. "Near here?"

"The Shell station over at Oakview Plaza," she said.

"Hey, I've stopped there," he said with something like enthusiasm in his voice. "That old guy's your dad?"

"Uh-huh," she said. "I used to help out there all the time when I was little."

"That's weird," he said grinning. "Most girls I know don't know one end of a car from the other. Too bad your dad's station isn't closer."

Pam nodded. "It is pretty far if you're about to boil over."

He was still looking at her as if he didn't quite believe what was going on. "You know anything about this place Bradley's?"

"Anyone can check a thermostat for you, I guess," Pam said. "And if it's the radiator, they'll have to send it out anyway." Her gaze drifted out the window to the car. "That's a nice car your friend has."

He looked out of the window and beamed. "Yeah," he said. Then he straightened up. "Well, I guess I'll give Bradley's a try then." He began to walk toward the door. "See ya around," he said. "Maybe I'll stop by your old man's station."

"See you," Pam said.

The door swung shut behind him.

Pam was staring after him. "Wow," she said. "How about that?"

"I was impressed," I said. "My best friend actually told a Hell's Angel how to take care of a car! And I think he was as impressed as I was."

"You think so?" she asked. "Wasn't he incredible?"

"Incredibly scary," I said. "I sure wouldn't want to get on his bad side."

"I think he was interesting," she said. "And exciting, too."

"You liked him?"

"Uh-huh," she said, blushing.

"No kidding?" I said, amazed. "Next thing I know you'll be spending all your spare time up at your dad's station, just in case he comes in."

"What spare time?" she asked, then sighed. "All I ever do is watch Grandma. Which reminds me"— she checked her watch—"I have to get back. I told my mom I'd only be gone for an hour, which is probably my time off for the entire summer."

"You have to have some time to yourself this summer," I said. "You worked hard all school year."

"It's okay," she said, looking down at the remains of her sundae. "It's not too pleasant at my house right now, but I'll be all right. It's not as if I had anything else special to do."

"You could hang around the Shell station and wait for Mr. Leather-and-Chains to stop by."

She shrugged. "He'll forget me in a day and a half. Let's face it, Debbie, I'm not the sort of girl that guys remember, except for my mechanical ability."

"That's a big advantage," I said. "Most girls don't know a thing about cars. And most boys love their cars more than any girl. You should have a head start with guys."

"Some head start," she said. "The only guys who notice me in school are the ones who want help with their homework, or who bump into me in the halls." She played with the corner of her napkin, tearing it into neat little rows. "It's never bugged me too much before. You know me—I'm a fairly happy person. I like being alone and reading and things. It's just that now, with all this going on at home, I'd really like to be special to someone."

"You've got me," I said.

She grinned. "No offense," she said, "but I meant someone of the opposite sex. Just once in my life I'd like to be the person who mattered most in the world to someone else. Preferably a someone else who's tall, dark, and handsome . . . or tall, fair, and handsome, or even tall, purple, and handsome. I'm not too fussy."

She made a funny face as she got to her feet. "Well, gotta go," she said. "Back to the spaghetti-dodging contest. See you, Deb. Here's money for the sundae."

"This one's on me," I said. "I just wish there was more I could do for you."

"Thanks," she said. "I'm glad I've got you anyway. Even if you're not a guy."

"Good. I'd do a lot of things for you, but that doesn't include becoming a boy."

She laughed and waved and ran out the door. I watched as her little Honda chugged past, and I couldn't help thinking wistfully back to last summer when I lived with two parents in a big house on the golf course and Pam had a grandmother who still baked cookies and our biggest problem was how to get an even tan on all sides of our legs.

Chapter 3 —————————

"**H**ey, Debbie, where is everybody?" Joe called when he arrived back at the café an hour or so later. He stood there in the doorway, his mop of dark curls still windswept from his motorcycle ride, his leather jacket slung over one shoulder. "Don't tell me you poisoned them all with your cooking again."

"Ha, ha, very funny," I cleverly retorted. "It's so nice out, they're probably all still down at the beach."

"Oh, I thought one of Howard's horror movies had finally come true and Rockley Beach had been zapped into another dimension," he said.

"What a horrible fate—being trapped in another dimension with you," I quipped.

"Could be worse," he said smoothly, and eyed me in his cool, confident way, which always made me uneasy.

"Anyway, what took you so long?" I asked. "I

didn't think any doctor saw his patients for more than fifteen minutes these days."

"I had to get Poppa back to bed," he said. "He gets so upset every time he talks to doctors that he has to take a nap afterward. I came back as fast as I could. Anything happen while I was away?"

"Nothing much, except you missed a visit from a certain special somebody," I said mysteriously.

"Really, who?"

"Let me give you a hint," I said. I tossed my hair, fluttered my eyelashes, and said in a breathy voice, "Joe's not here? Oh, rats!"

I saw the corners of his mouth flicker upward in a smile before he caught himself. "I take it you mean Wendy was here," he said.

"Very good," I said.

"What did she want?"

"She wouldn't entrust that sort of information to a mere waitress like me," I said. "She said she'd call you later."

"Okay," he said. He took his uniform jacket out of the closet and began to put it on. "She's, er, something else, isn't she?" he asked casually.

"Oh, yes, you could definitely say that," I agreed. "Definitely something else."

There was a pause while he stood with his back to me and buttoned his jacket.

"You two got along okay?" he asked.

"We didn't have much opportunity," I said smoothly. "She left as soon as she found out you weren't here. Oh, and she had no idea who I was."

"Really? I know I've told her about you."

"Maybe I wasn't important enough to remember."

"Wendy's really a very sweet person," he said, obviously feeling as if he had to defend her. "She's very warm."

"I don't doubt it," I said with a grin.

"She'd feel very out of place down here," he went on. "I wonder what she wanted."

"Probably she was feeling unappreciated and came here so you'd make a fuss and tell her how *gorg*eous she is. Positive reinforcement, you know."

"Positive what?"

"Oh, did I use a big word?" I asked sweetly, knowing it would make Joe mad. "I forgot about your limited vocabulary."

"Wendy never criticizes my vocabulary," he countered.

"No, well, she wouldn't, would she? Her own is limited to oohs and aahs and the occasional 'Oh, rats!' "

"She's much more expressive when we're alone," he said triumphantly, cocking an eyebrow lewdly.

"I don't want to hear about it." I shook the lettuce I was washing so violently that water splattered all over the room.

"Hey, watch it, will you," he muttered. "I already showered today."

"What's the occasion? I'll write it on the calendar!"

"Very funny," he growled. "How about getting

that lettuce cut up and in the bin instead of throwing it around?"

"How about you getting back to work rather than just standing there watching me?" I countered.

He smiled easily, leaning against the doorframe.

"I'm the boss around here, remember. I don't have to take orders from the hired help!"

"Wrong," I reminded him, taking the next batch of lettuce and shaking it wildly. "Your grandfather is out of the hospital now, remember? That means you're only the assistant boss."

"I'm still the boss over you," he said. "And will you cut that out?"

I grinned. "Oh, sorry," I said, putting down the damp lettuce. "I didn't notice. Did I get your hair wet?"

"You know darn well you did," he said, trying to look angry but grinning at the same time.

"Well, excuuuuse me," I countered. "I guess I'm just so exhausted, trying to do everything alone, I can't control my arms any longer."

"In that case, come over here," Joe said, giving me a very provocative look. "I guess you won't be able to fight me off."

"I'll find enough strength for that," I said quickly, but my eyes held his for a second. There had been a couple of crazy times when I was mixed up about my family and boys and the state of life in general and I hadn't wanted to fight Joe Garbarini off. He obviously remembered them as vividly as I did.

"So where is everybody really?" Joe repeated after I went back to my work and refused to flirt with him any longer.

"I don't know," I said. "I guess Art's out surfing, and he's probably got Josh and Brett with him."

"Not Josh," Joe said. "He's working."

"Josh has a job?" I asked, surprised. Art and his friends were all total beach bums, ready to bum money off any of the other customers. They were only interested in how good the waves were and how many cute girls were on the beach.

Joe looked equally shocked. "In a factory, loading boxes. Can you imagine?" he asked. "Man, I'd rather starve."

"Some of us have to take any job we can get," I said. "Look at me. Last summer I spent every day lounging around the pool at the country club sipping iced tea."

"Yeah, well . . ." Joe's face split into a broad grin. "You've really joined the real world, haven't you?" he said. "Anyhow, in your case it's different. You'd rather be here."

"Says who?" I demanded. "You think it's more fun scrubbing tables and cooking french fries than hanging out at a pool?"

Joe looked smug. "You're mixing with more fun people," he said.

"Like who?"

"Like me, for one. I mean, compared to that creepy android you used to date . . . Hey, you were dying of boredom, right?"

"Did anyone ever tell you you were conceited?" I asked.

"You do, about a thousand times a day."

"And you haven't changed," I said. "Which proves what I've always thought."

"Which is?"

"That you're a slow learner," I said, smiling and drawing an invisible "1" in the air. One point for me.

Joe obviously recognized that I'd scored a point, too. His face became suddenly serious again. "Get that french fryer going, woman," Joe said. "We haven't got all day."

"Oh, you're right," I agreed. "It's much more fun here! Working eight hours a day in a three-hundred-degree kitchen, lovely, greasy french fryer to play with, nice dirty floors to scrub, scintillating conversation with Mr. Teenage Heartthrob of America—I can't think why I wasted all my summers until now sunbathing at the country club with my friends. In fact, I—*yowww*!"

I broke off with a yelp as something cold slipped down my back. I spun around to Joe. "What was that?"

"An ice cube! I thought you'd be pining for the iced tea you mentioned, and I wanted to make you feel at home!" he said, grinning delightedly.

"You creep! It's freezing!"

"Ice usually is. See, I know all that scientific stuff, and you thought I was a moron."

I wriggled, trying to shake the ice cube loose, but it was stuck firmly at the belt of my uniform dress. "It's horrible. Get it out!"

"If you say so," Joe said, innocently slipping a hand down the back of my dress.

"No, you creep!" I said, grabbing his hand.

"I thought you wanted me to help. Just like a

woman—can't make up her mind!" he said, trying
to stop laughing while I glared at him.

"I'm going to the ladies' room," I said with as
much dignity as I could manage. "If anyone needs
me, I'll be removing a horrible, cold ice cube that
some uncivilized caveman with a brain the size of
a pea put down my back."

I swept from the room. Joe burst out laughing,
but I managed not to turn around.

"That guy is going too far!" I muttered to myself
as I stood in the girls' bathroom and shook the ice
cube loose. "He doesn't know when to stop."

Then I realized that I, too, might be just slightly
to blame. Maybe I didn't know any better when to
stop. I should never have let Joe take me home
that night when I broke up with Grant, I told myself. But then, I reasoned, I hadn't been in any state
to take myself home. I had drunk a little too much
champagne, and Joe had rescued me. He drove me
home, and I . . . I turned away from the mirror,
unable to look at my own face any longer. I begged
him to stay. He hadn't stayed, of course, but since
that night it was as if an invisible barrier had been
removed from between us. We still fought, we still
teased, but sometimes he looked at me as if we
shared a special secret, and sometimes I found myself thinking about him and what it would have
been like if he hadn't gone home.

This is crazy! I said to myself. *We have absolutely nothing in common. He is Mr. Macho in person! And besides, it's pointless to think about it,
because Joe's got Wendy.*

And I had nobody. I'd broken up with Grant, I

no longer had a two-parent family or lived in the country club, and I didn't really fit in with the people at the café.

I kicked the ice cube across the floor, and it thudded against the tiled wall. I rebuttoned my belt, straightened my hair, and left the bathroom. Joe greeted me with a smug little grin. "Hey, look, it's Frosty the Snowman," he called.

"Very amusing," I said. "Most witty. If you don't need me around here, I'll go lie on the beach. It's a beautiful day."

"It's almost evening," he said. "That's why I can't understand why we don't have more customers. Ashley's not even here yet. She always comes in for a soda around this time."

"You should be grateful," I said. "At least we're not being run off our feet anymore like we were when they were shooting that dumb movie."

Earlier in the summer, a movie had been made in Rockley Beach, and the Heartbreak was one of the locations they used. The café was packed with hopeful movie stars the whole time the film crew was there.

Joe looked up with a frown. "I figured business would pick up because of the movie. I thought everyone would want to see where it was shot."

"I'm sure they will, once the movie comes out and they see the Heartbreak in it," I said, "but right now I'm glad we can take it easy. I'm glad things are back to normal here."

As I spoke the front door burst open and loud voices carried to the kitchen.

"This is just plain dumb, Ashley. It just isn't possible!" Howard, our resident science-fiction nerd, sounded so mad his voice was barely a squeak.

"Is, too. I read it in the papers, so it must be true."

"Not if it was in the sort of papers you read. They're full of garbage."

"They are not!"

Joe and I hurried out of the kitchen. Ashley and Howard were facing each other defiantly. After the incredible things she had worn to try to get into the movie, Ashley looked almost subdued. She had on a white miniskirt, very short, a purple halter top, and a wooden necklace made of huge carved jungle animals. The zebra and giraffe danced against each other with a loud clacking noise as Ashley shook her finger at Howard. Her hair was no longer teased out like a bird's nest, but instead hung long and jet black, half obscuring her face. Howard's hair was buzzed short and stuck up like toothbrush bristles about his moon face, and with his thick-framed glasses, it made him look extra nerdy. His T-shirt read: "Have You Written to Your Mummy Lately?" and had a picture of an Egyptian tomb on it.

Joe stepped between them. "Hey, guys, cool it. What's the problem?" he asked.

"I was just being nice," Ashley said with her famous pout. "I just told him a surefire way to win at his dumb old computer games, and he's not interested."

"Because it's baloney, Ashley. It's just not possible," Howard shouted.

"I read it," Ashley explained to me and Joe. "I read it in the newspaper."

Ashley was famous for reading all the supermarket tabloids and for believing everything in them.

Howard's face was bright pink. He turned to us for help. "She keeps trying to tell me that you can beat the computer," he began to explain.

"If you play it long enough, it gets tired," Ashley explained as if she were talking to a two-year-old. "I keep telling him, but he won't listen. It's so simple. You just keep playing the same game, and in the end the computer gets tired and then you win."

Joe and I glanced at each other. Howard's face was now almost purple. "And I keep telling her that you can't make computers tired," he shouted back. "Computers are little silicon chips. Chips do not get tired. They can play the same game forever and ever."

"Why don't you try it and see, Howard?" Ashley demanded. "Try it and you'll see I'm right!"

"Make her understand, Joe," Howard pleaded.

Joe looked at me and grinned. "Things are back to normal all right."

Chapter 4 ——————————

*J*oe must have totally jinxed us when he complained that the Heartbreak was empty because that weekend was one of the craziest we had had all summer. As well as our regular beach crowd, the place was packed with tourists. I think they must have unloaded a few sight-seeing buses around the corner and sent them all to us. We were run ragged trying to keep up with orders. Mr. Garbarini was delighted, of course, because of all the money we took in, but Joe and I were not so thrilled. I reminded them both, more than once, that they had promised to hire another waitress so that Joe and I could get a day off once in a while.

By Sunday night I was completely exhausted. I was almost asleep when I remembered that Pam had not shown up at the café all weekend. She had said that she would when I talked to her on Friday night, and I had been so busy that I had forgotten about her. I felt bad about it right away. She had been great to me when I was in midcrisis and needed someone to talk to. I couldn't let her down now, when she obviously needed a friend. It was still early, so I woke myself up and called her.

"I thought you were going to come down to the café and say hi," I said when she answered the phone. "Or did you decide not to come in when you saw how crowded it was?"

"I couldn't get away," she said. "It hasn't been the greatest weekend of my life, actually. My parents went to my sister's gymnastics competition, and I was stuck with my grandmother."

"That's too bad."

"It's more than too bad," she said sharply—and Pam never spoke sharply to anyone. "I don't think you understand at all, Debbie! You know how I used to love Grandma. She used to bake cookies and do all those other grandmothery sort of things, and now she doesn't even know who I am! She thinks I'm her sister who died, and she says the most horrible things to me."

"I'm really sorry," I said. "It must be terrible for you. It's hard when people you love change and you suddenly don't know them at all. I went through the same thing when my father moved out and started trying to 'find' himself."

"At least your father's alive and healthy," Pam said with a big sigh, as if it weren't the same thing at all. "At least you know he'll probably calm down and become your father again. My grandmother will never get any better. She'll never remember me again. She'll die hating me."

"I'm sure she won't," I said gently. "She doesn't hate you, Pam. It's just that her brain has you mixed up with someone else right now. Maybe when she's in the home, things will get better."

"I hope so," Pam said, "because I don't know how much more of this I can take." There was a long pause. "I know one thing," she said at last. "I don't seem to matter to anyone anymore. Everyone only has time for looking after Grandma."

"Isn't that sort of understandable? She needs a lot of supervision right now."

"Except that they had time to go to my sister's meet this weekend," she said bleakly. "I think they've forgotten I exist."

"Oh, Pam, you know that's not true," I said. "They're treating you like another adult because you're so responsible. Your sister's still a little kid."

"Then why was I the one who got thrown out of her room and had to share with Janine?" she asked. "Why didn't they make Janine move in with me? I don't even have a place of my own. Janine's always saying, 'Don't touch my toys. Don't sit there. It's my room, remember?' "

"Janine always was a pain," I agreed. Never having had a sister, I couldn't really imagine what it was like to have to share anything, but I did know what it was like to be ignored at home. My mother, busy with her new life back in school, had had very little time for me recently. I'd gotten used to letting myself into an empty house, to fixing my own meals and washing my own clothes, but it had been very hard for me at first.

"It won't last forever," I said. "And you've still got me. You can call me whenever you want to."

"You're never home," she said, trying to laugh.

"Then come down to the Heartbreak. It will take your mind off things."

"I just don't feel like being around people," she said. "When I see everyone having a great time, I just get more depressed. Especially when it seems like everyone else in the world except me has a date."

"I'm dateless, too, remember?" I asked.

"By choice," she said, "and you have Joe around."

"Big deal."

"Joe is a big deal, you just won't admit it."

"Please say you'll come down to the café," I said, changing the subject. "We've been swamped with cute guys this weekend."

"Cute guys?"

"Lots of them," I assured her. "All the cute surfers, for one, and the vacationers and weekenders from the city who try to talk surfer talk."

"That does sound tempting," she agreed. "Not that any of them would notice me."

"Who knows," I said. "Maybe this is your lucky summer. Maybe fate is waiting for you at the Heartbreak Cafe."

Pam laughed. "I guess it couldn't hurt."

"Great. It'll be good for you, and even if you don't meet the guy of your dreams, we can have some laughs together. You would have laughed if you'd heard Ashley and Howard arguing over how to trick a computer this afternoon. Oh, and we had a couple of German tourists in today—big, blond guys with huge muscles—and one of them said, 'I was making zee holding on ten, no?' "

"The what?"

"He meant hang ten," I explained. "He was trying to master surfer talk. Art said he was a menace out there with a board he couldn't control. He asked me to teach him English. His name's Klaus and his friend's name is Peter."

There was a pause while Pam digested this. "Klaus and Peter?" she asked. "Big and blond, with muscles?"

"That's right, and funny, too. Maybe we could give them a little English tutoring together if they show up again—although I don't know if they are exactly your type. Intellectually they are not Albert Einstein."

"Who cares about intellect?" Pam replied. "How do they look in swimsuits?"

"Pam Paulson, I'm surprised at you!" I said, trying to sound shocked. "Is this the same girl that was given the distinguished science award at school, and the foreign-language book award?"

"And look where it's gotten me," Pam said with a sigh. "A lonely old maid of sixteen going on seventeen who has never had a real date."

I could sense that this conversation was rapidly slipping back into the depressing mode.

"Look, I've got a great idea," I said. "How about if you come down to the café tomorrow? I'll take some time off in the afternoon and we'll go guy watching on the beach. Joe's been coming in late and he owes me some time. And it's not like we're super busy during the day anyway. So what do you say?"

"It does sound tempting," Pam said. "I'll see if they can spare me."

"You deserve a little time off," I insisted. "Tell them I said so."

"I deserve a lot of things," Pam said slowly, "but I don't seem to be getting them."

"Maybe tomorrow will be the beginning of bigger and better things."

"I hope so. You're the best, Deb," she added, which made me feel happy and warm.

"Promise you'll show up tomorrow?" I insisted.

"You sure know how to convince a person," Pam said. "Okay. I'll really try to come. What should I wear?" She sounded nervous again, as if this were a date and not just hanging out at a café. "I mean, Joe will be there, won't he? And those German guys. I wonder what is *in* in Germany."

"I can't guarantee that the Germans will show up again," I said, "but wear your new blue sundress. You look really good in that."

"I look slightly better than blah in that," she said. "Still, maybe Joe will smile at me and say hi, which would make my summer. . . ."

"You need a quick course in self-confidence, young woman," I said sternly. "I think we'll start right away. Come over to my place before we go down to the café, and I'll give you my famous beauty treatment."

"Not the facial pack you tried on me once?" she asked, sounding hesitant. "You remember, you mashed up all those avocados and cucumbers and things and I ended up smelling like a salad all night?"

I giggled. "That was one of my few failures," I said. "But we can raid my mom's stuff. She's really into recapturing her lost youth these days."

"I think your mom looks good," Pam said loyally. "I think she looks pretty young anyway. I bet she has lots of guys who are interested in her at college."

"My mom?" I asked, and giggled again. "Dating? Get real. This guy did come over to help her with her homework, but that is the extent of her romantic activities."

"All the same," Pam said, "she'll have to start dating sometime, won't she?"

"I guess," I said slowly. "That is, if she and my dad don't get back together."

"You think that's a possibility?" she asked.

"No, I guess not," I admitted.

"Well, I've gotta go," Pam said. "My mom's yelling. I think Grandma's out of bed again. See you tomorrow, okay?"

"Okay," I said. "See you tomorrow!" I put down the phone slowly. In the mirror I could see my forehead was wrinkled with worry lines.

Life was suddenly so complicated. Pam and I had both had to grow up in a hurry. Whenever I started thinking about the future these days, I got scared. I hadn't even considered my mother dating and even marrying someone else before then, and I wished Pam hadn't brought it up. I didn't want to think of it. Even her doing her homework with Norman had worried me, and nobody could have been more harmless than he was. A part of me still kept hoping that my parents would get back together again and that everything would be the way it was before.

"Think positive, that's what you just told Pam," I said to myself. Right now my number-one priority was not worrying about myself but making sure my best friend got a break from all her problems. I wished I could really make good things start to happen to her—get her away from the sad situation at home, even find her a cute guy of her own. She just needed some confidence and the right moment, I thought. I wished I had a magic wand so I could wave it and make things go well for her!

Chapter 5 _____

*T*he trouble with wishing is that sometimes you get what you wish for. Pam had hardly arrived at the café the next day after a makeover session at my house—I styled her hair in a sleek French braid and made her up to accent her eyes and define her cheekbones—when a group of kids came in. I had just settled her at a table next to Howard, who liked to trade horror-movie reviews with her, when I heard the front door open. Loud laughter filled the café.

"Jeez, it's like a morgue in here," I heard one person complain. "Where is everybody?"

"Are these kids alive?" someone else joined in. "Hey, you, are you alive? Yeah, you!"

The voices sounded so menacing that my first thought was that Art and his surfing buddies were putting us on again. They were always acting like weirdos if any tourists were in the café. But I came out of the kitchen to find that it wasn't Art, or anyone like him. It was a group of kids I'd never seen before—kids who matched their menacing voices. They were the sort of toughs I'd first imagined Joe to be; their leather jackets studded and painted with eagles and motorcycle logos, their tight jeans ripped at the knees. A couple of girls were with them, and they looked tough, too, with loads of bright makeup and studded leather jackets of their own. The group looked around coolly like they were trying to decide what to make of the café.

One of my nightmares had just come true. When I had first started working at the café, I often wondered what I'd do if a group like this came in late at night when I was alone. Most of the time Joe or his grandfather was around and I didn't have to worry. They were both capable of dealing with any trouble. But sometimes, when Joe sneaked out early on a date and left me to close up, I'd wonder how I'd handle a situation like this. It wasn't the middle of the night now, but somehow that made the group even more scary. I glanced back at the phone on the wall and wondered how fast I could dial 911.

Maybe I'm overreacting, I told myself calmly. *Maybe they are just passing through and they're thirsty like anyone else.*

I swallowed hard and straightened my cap as I came out of the kitchen.

"Hi, can I help you?" I heard myself say, my voice unnaturally bright.

The tallest member of the group, a big bear of a guy with a mop of unruly hair, a shaggy beard, and an earring in one ear, turned toward me. "Who are you?" he asked.

"Debbie. I work here," I said.

"Where's Joe?"

"He's, er, not in yet," I said, and immediately wished I hadn't. Why couldn't I have said that he was out and would be back right away, or out for a walk with his friend the policeman? Anything to make them think that I wasn't there all alone.

The tall dark guy's eyes flickered. "You're here alone, then?" he asked.

"That's right," I said. "Joe should be in later if you want to come back."

One of the girls tugged at the big guy's arm. "I'm thirsty, Danny," she said. "Let's get something to drink, okay?"

The big guy shook her off. "What time is it?" he asked.

"Just after two," I said, praying that they had an urgent appointment on the other side of the country by two-thirty.

Danny exchanged glances with another of the boys—a leaner, more catlike, longer-haired version of Joe. "We better wait here for Matt and Spike, right?"

"Right," the other boy agreed. "They said to meet them here."

He made it sound as if the reason for meeting Matt and Spike, whoever they were, was not to play checkers with them.

Great, I thought, giving Pam a worried look, *they were about to have a gang war in the café!*

The skinny guy turned to me. "You know Terry from the auto shop?" he asked.

"Sure."

"Has he been in yet today?"

"Not since I got here," I answered. Somehow this guy came across as one level more civilized than his friends.

He looked around in a bored sort of way, then nodded to the big guy. "We'll wait," he said. They began to walk to the back of the café and settled themselves at the round table next to Howard and Pam. They cringed, but the leather-jacket gang didn't even appear to have seen them.

"Terry's been working on Matt's car," one of the other boys confided. He was at the back of the group, not so wildly dressed, obviously someone's sidekick. "He's real good with souping up engines."

"Yes, he is," I answered, amazed that I was actually having the conversation.

"You ever see us play?" he went on.

"Play?"

"Spike and Danny and the group?" another one put in. "They're called the Road Warriors—you know, heavy metal. They play all the clubs."

"I don't go to clubs much," I said.

"You can bring us all sodas," one of the girls commanded.

"What do you got to eat?" Danny demanded. "I'm hungry."

I was so nervous I had this absurd desire to giggle, to say something like, "Sorry, we don't serve brontosaurus burgers here." I ignored it and said,

"Burgers, hot dogs, fries. And then there's all our desserts—we make a great chocolate madness."

I saw the guy's eyes flicker with interest. "A chocolate madness, oh, my," he said, his voice high and teasing. "How about that, guys? Do you serve cappuccino and croissants, too?"

"Just ordinary coffee," I said, fighting the blush that was creeping across my face. "You'd have to go to the cafés on the beach for that."

Danny continued to grin at me. "Looks like you belong down there, too. What are you doing here?"

"Hey, maybe she's Joe's latest," another boy commented.

I was torn between agreeing with him to get them instantly off my back, and denying it. For once I decided that Joe was the lesser of two evils. I didn't want these guys to think I was boyfriend-less and unprotected. "I, er, might be," I said, giving my most mysterious smile.

It worked instantly. Joe was the sort of guy that other boys respected and didn't mess with.

"I'll have a burger and fries," the friendly boy who had spoken to me before said.

"Me, too."

"Just fries for me."

I took orders from the entire group. I glanced over at Howard and Pam as I walked back to the kitchen.

"If you'd like to go on down to the beach, I'll join you a little later," I suggested to Pam, but she shook her head. "No, thanks, this is interesting," she whispered. "I feel like an anthropologist observing a primitive tribe."

"I hope they don't become too primitive to handle," I muttered back.

She shook her head again. "This is all just an act, don't you see? They're trying to make a statement."

I gave her a sideways glance as I hurried back to the kitchen. You could take scientific detachment too far, I thought. I personally would not like to be sitting at the table next to a heavy-metal group that looked as if they smashed up furniture and ate it for breakfast!

I cooked everything in record time and carried the plates out with incredible efficiency. It's amazing what you can do when fear makes the adrenaline flow! I noticed that either they had calmed down or they weren't as bad as I first thought, because they were talking and laughing harmlessly about fast cars and drag racing and outrunning the cops. I was just on my way to their table, plates balanced on both arms and praying that I wouldn't do anything dumb like trip over a chair and spill them all, when the front door opened again.

One member of the heavy metal group shouted, "Hey, it's Spike. We waited for you."

"You get Matt's car?" a girl called.

"Yeah. No problem," he said, and began to walk across to them. "Matt went home, though."

"We're just about to eat," Danny, the big guy, said, his eye roving across to me, still standing with plates balanced on my arms. "If the food ever gets here."

Mechanically I crossed the room and began to put plates in front of people. They all moved over

to make room for Spike. The way they talked to
him eagerly made it clear that he was the leader,
and the way he sat, sprawling out his long legs
across the aisle, made it clear that he knew it.

"Can I get you something?" I asked. I looked at
him clearly for the first time and realized there
was something definitely familiar about him. I tried
to remember where I'd seen him. He ordered a
soda. As I went to get it Pam grabbed at me.

"It's him," she whispered. "You remember. He
came in here with car trouble?" Her face was
flushed.

"That's right, and you talked about car engines
with him," I said, and gave her a nervous grin.
"You can remind him of that if they begin smash-
ing up the place."

"I'm sure he's really very nice," Pam said, and
flushed a little pinker.

I went to get Spike's drink and was in the kitchen
when things erupted again. A voice growled loudly.
"Hey, there's no ketchup in this bottle! Get me another ketchup. This thing is empty!"

"No, it's not. Here, let me do it. You got to hit it
good, like this," came a second voice. I came running in in time to see Danny give the ketchup bottle a swift thump. A great stream of red liquid sailed
through the air, right onto Pam's dress. For a moment there was silence, as if everyone in the café
were frozen in time. Then Pam leaped up, looking
down at the ugly red splotch on her side.

"Oh, no," she said calmly, still maintaining her
typical cool even though the dress was her newest
and favorite.

"Look what you've done, Danny!" one of the girls yelled, but she was grinning.

"Well, sorry!" he said. "They should make ketchup that comes out of bottles easily. Wasn't my fault!"

The other girl returned at that exact moment from the ladies' room, took one look at Pam, and screamed. "She got stabbed?"

"No, dummy!"

"Shot?"

"No!"

"But look at all that blood! Someone get a doctor!"

Howard was already trying to wipe away the ketchup with napkins, and Pam was trying to stop him because all he was doing was spreading the stain around more.

"Listen, dumbo, it's only ketchup!" Danny sneered. "But I guess if Miss Harpooned Whale here is your girlfriend . . . Rough life, isn't it, Poindexter?"

The group broke into noisy laughter again. I saw Pam's face go bright red, and I stepped forward to intervene. Before I could do anything, though, Howard turned to face Danny. "I don't think that's at all amusing. Don't you dare insult her like that!" he said in his funny, squeaky voice.

"Or what?" Danny asked, grinning.

"Or you'll have me to deal with," Howard said. "I know karate, you know."

He started to wave his arms, making Japanesey sounds in his throat. Danny reached out a massive hand and grabbed Howard's shirtfront. Howard made ineffective chopping movements, but he couldn't get to Danny. Danny laughed out loud and lifted Howard clean off his feet. "Oh, I am really scared," he said in a voice dripping with sarcasm. "Please don't hit me, Mr. Nerd, you might put a crease in my shirt!"

The others in the group were adding insults as they laughed. I could sense that the situation was getting out of hand, and I hesitated between rushing in to help and slipping back to call the police. But before I could act, Pam put herself between Howard and Danny. She gave Danny a shove that he wasn't expecting, which threw him off balance. He staggered backward into the table, breaking his grip on Howard.

"Pick on someone your own size, you bully," she said angrily. "In fact why don't you pick on someone with your own size brain. I think we have a couple of worms in the backyard you could take on. Or there are some jellyfish lying on the beach today!"

Everyone laughed. Danny's face turned red. "Maybe you should go back to your cave until you know how civilized people behave," Pam went on while everyone else was too surprised to do anything. "A civilized human being would apologize when he ruined someone's clothing, not start insulting!"

"Now you just watch your mouth, girl," Danny began, but then Spike stood up.

"Cool it, Danny," he said quietly. "She's right. You should apologize." He turned to Pam. "Look,

I'm sorry if he ruined your dress," he said. "It was an accident. Will it wash off?"

"I, er, don't know," Pam stammered. "Maybe if I washed it before the ketchup dried."

They stared at each other. "I met you here last time," he said. "You were the one who said it might be the thermostat. You were right."

"Was I? How about that," she answered.

They continued to stand there.

"You live near here?" Spike asked.

"A couple of miles," Pam said.

"I'll drive you home if you want," Spike said.

"But your friends—"

"They can wait. My car's right outside," he said. "We can be there and back in ten minutes."

Pam hesitated, then smiled shyly. "Okay, thanks," she said. Spike turned to his friends, who were looking as astounded as I was.

"I'll be back," he said, then turned and walked to the door. Pam followed him. I stepped up to stop her.

"Look, Pam, you could wash your dress off here," I said.

"It's okay," she said calmly. "I'll be fine. See you later."

Then they both disappeared, and seconds later I heard a car roar off. I think I almost held my breath for the next half hour—until the car returned. Spike came back in, but no Pam.

"Where is Pam?" I demanded, my nerves stretched tighter than a violin string.

"She decided to stay home," he said. "She said she'll call you later."

Terry appeared almost immediately, and the whole group went off with him. As soon as the door was closed behind them I rushed to the phone.

"Pfhew, I'm so glad to hear your voice," I said when Pam answered. "I thought you might be lying in a ditch somewhere by now. What on earth made you go off with *him*?"

"What's wrong with him?" Pam asked innocently. "I think he's gorgeous, and he was so nice about my dress."

"I have to admit that amazed me," I said. "Totally out of character."

"I don't know," she said slowly. "Remember what I said about all this tough stuff being an act? I bet they're all really nice. They probably just want attention."

I laughed nervously. "That's not how they came across to me," I said, "although I have to admit Spike seemed a little more civilized than the rest."

Howard came up behind me, appearing from nowhere in his unnerving way and breathing down my neck. "Is that Pam?" he asked.

"Uh-huh." I nodded, trying to listen to Pam at the other end of the line.

"Has she been kidnapped?" Howard whispered in my ear. "Is she being held hostage?"

"He's nice," Pam was saying. "I really like him, Deb."

"Is she all right?" Howard asked. "Is she calling from jail? She's not hacked to pieces, is she? Is she lying stabbed in a hospital bed? Was she in the middle of a shoot-out?"

"No!" I shouted. "Oh, not you, Pam. I'm talking to Howard. Go ahead, please."

"What was his problem?" Pam asked.

"He was worried about you, that's all."

"Tell him not to worry, although I think that's very sweet of him. Tell him Spike is really very nice. Hey, guess what? Did you know he plays in a band—a real rock band at real clubs and everything? He told me while he was driving me home."

"That's great," I said. "Just don't go falling for anyone like him, will you?"

"I, er, think I already have," she said.

"But, Pam," I began, "he's not your type!"

"You mean he's not from the country club? I thought you were over that stage."

"You know I don't mean that!" I said sharply.

"So what is my type?" Pam asked fiercely.

"You know, someone thoughtful and intellectual. Someone like you, Pam."

"I've been waiting sixteen whole years for some guy to notice me," she said. "And look where it's got me! I've never had a real date, and I'm going to be a senior. That's just great, isn't it? Before I know it, I'll be through college and living alone with cats."

I laughed nervously. "Come on, Pam, don't get carried away. You may never see him again."

"Which is where you are wrong," Pam said, "because he asked me to go to a movie with him tonight."

"No k-kidding?" I stammered. "Are you sure?"

"Well, he said, 'Want to go to a movie tonight?'

which I took to mean did I want to go to a movie tonight."

There was a long pause. "You're not going to go, are you?" I finally asked.

"I don't see why not," she said.

"I can think of a hundred reasons," I said. "You've had no experience with boys, you're not equipped to handle a guy like that, Pam."

"Like what?"

"You know. You've heard what these rock bands are like. Besides, he looks like a real smoothie. What if he tries something in the car on the way home?"

"I think you've got him all wrong, Debbie," Pam said. "He really isn't as bad as you think."

"I still think you should have your head examined," I said bluntly.

"That's a chance I have to take," she said, "and right now I'm prepared to take it. He might just be the guy I've been waiting for."

"A tough who drag-races and plays heavy metal is the guy you've been waiting for?" I asked angrily.

"Hey, listen to me," she said, equally angrily. "I've never had a boyfriend before, remember? At least this guy noticed me and stuck up for me and drove me home. If he's a bit different from the kids I've known until now, so what? If you ask me, it's kind of exciting."

"Okay, Pam, if you're sure you know what you're doing," I said.

"I'm not sure," she said, "but there's not much else that's fun or exciting in my life right now."

She paused. "Besides, I'm only going to a movie with the guy. I didn't promise to run away with him to Casablanca, did I?"

I laughed. "No, you didn't. And don't think I want to spoil your fun. I do want you to be happy. I just don't want you to find yourself in a situation you can't handle."

"I think I can handle this," she said. "In fact, I have a good feeling about it, so don't worry, okay?"

"Okay," I said. "Call me as soon as you get back from the movie and let me know all about it."

She laughed. "You're worse than my mom," she said. "Although these days she wouldn't even notice if I was home or not, and wouldn't even care if I went out with King Kong."

"Come on, Pam," I said. "You know they really care about you. They're just going through tough times, remember? That's what you told me when I felt my folks were ignoring me."

"I guess so," she said. "Anyway, I'll call you if I'm not home too late."

"And be good," I said.

"Or I'll turn into a pumpkin at midnight?" she asked, laughing. "Actually, I do feel a little like Cinderella. Household slave rescued by unknown handsome prince."

"I hope he turns out to be a prince and not a frog," I said to myself as I hung up.

Chapter 6 _____

*P*am didn't call me that evening. I dozed off with the phone on my bed beside me and woke around two to realize that I hadn't heard from her. I was awake for the rest of the night worrying about her, trying to reason with myself that if she hadn't come home, her parents would have checked with me first. Then I worried that she had slipped out without telling them and they didn't even know she was missing and not safely in her own bed. As the night wore on and I got more and more tired, the scenario became worse and worse. In my mind I went through every terrible thing that could have happened to her, tortured by guilt that I had let her go.

You don't own her, I kept telling myself. *You can't run her life. You warned her, and she chose not to take your warning. You did all you could do.* But somehow this didn't make me feel much better. A true best friend would have locked Pam in her room, stolen her clothes, or tied her up

52

rather than let her take her life in her hands with a strange and dangerous guy.

Toward dawn I finally fell asleep. I woke again feeling stupid and grouchy, when I heard my mother bustling around the kitchen. Even though it was only eight o'clock, I dialed Pam's number. Pam's mother answered, yelled for Pam, and after a very long pause a sleepy voice murmured, "Hello?"

"Pam, it's me," I said.

"Debbie? Is something wrong?"

"That's what I wanted to find out from you."

"What do you mean? It's only eight o'clock in the morning," she mumbled. "I'm still three-quarters asleep."

"Pam, I was worried about you. You didn't call last night."

"Oh, sorry about that," she said. "I didn't think you'd appreciate being woken at one. I was going to call you this morning."

"I was awake all night worrying," I said. "You could have called anytime and I'd have been waiting."

Pam giggled. "You dummy," she said, "I told you there was nothing to worry about."

"So you actually had a good time with him?" I asked.

"I had a great time," she said. "We went to this movie about this rock group—a little noisy but exciting. And then we went on to Uncle Otto's. Remember that place?"

"The club? Down by the bus station?" I asked.

"That's it," she said. "It was fun. Crazy but fun.

Spike's band plays there on Fridays. I'm going down on Friday to hear him play. Want to come?"

"I, er, usually work on Fridays," I said. "I have to see if Joe can do without me."

"I'm sure Spike can get us in for free," she said. "I can't wait to hear him play."

Pam was so bubbling over with excitement that I felt like an old grouch. And my head was as thick as cotton after a sleepless night.

"So you really had a good time with him?" I repeated.

"I said I did," she said firmly. "In spite of the way he looks, he is really a nice guy, Deb. He's so funny. He made me laugh so much at the club and when he drives—it's almost like we're flying. His car isn't as outrageous as Matt's—the one that broke down—but it still goes pretty fast. I kept pinching myself all night. I couldn't believe it was happening to me." She sounded so dreamy. "We've got to get together, Deb, and go shopping. I have to get a wardrobe, quick. I stood out like a sore thumb at that club. I don't want Spike to feel embarrassed to be around me. Do you think I should splurge on a leather jacket?"

"Hey, hold on a minute," I interrupted. "Don't get carried away with this. Has he actually asked to see you again?"

"Well, not in so many words, but I know I'll see him," she said. "He's not the sort of guy who likes to be tied down to times and dates. He told me that. He's the sort who will just show up on the doorstep when he feels like it."

"Did it ever occur to you that he was just being

nice last night, because he felt bad about his friends and because he felt sorry for you?" I asked.

"*No!*" she exploded. "That did not occur to me. He asked me out because he likes me, strange though that may seem to you. He said he's never met a girl who can talk about cars and racing with him before. Just because I don't happen to be thin and blond and pretty like you doesn't mean that one boy in the world can't find me attractive, you know."

"I know that," I said. "It's just that—"

"That a boy as cool looking as Spike couldn't be interested in a plain old chubbo like me?" she demanded.

"I didn't mean that at all."

"Then what did you mean?"

"He is a rock singer, Pam," I said slowly. Why did everything I tried to say keep coming out wrong? "And I guess he could have a whole lot of girls. I just don't want you to get the wrong idea about this and be let down if he doesn't call again."

"You sure are doing a lot to boost my self-confidence," she said coldly. "Not 'I'm glad you've got a great boy taking an interest in you, Pam,' but 'Remember that he only feels sorry for you and you'll never see him again because he couldn't possibly be interested in you.' I thought you were my best friend, Debbie."

"I am," I said miserably. "And you know I want the best for you. It's just that I'm scared for you, Pam. I don't want you to get hurt."

"I was getting hurt at home," she said. "I was getting hurt watching you dating Grant all year while I had nobody. This is the first really good time I've had in ages and you're trying to spoil it for me."

"Come on, Pam, you're usually the one who tells me not to rush into things and to consider both sides of situations. What exactly do you know about this guy, besides the fact that he drives fast cars and plays in a rock group? What school does he go to, for instance?"

"He, er, he's not going back to school in the fall."

"He's finished high school?"

"Er, no. He's, like, dropping out."

"Wonderful! You're one of the smartest kids at Oakview High and you're all set to fling yourself into the arms of a dropout."

"He has good reasons!" she said belligerently. "He says he can make so much money playing with the band that he doesn't need an education."

"You know that's dumb!" I exploded.

"Why are you going on at me like this?" Pam demanded. "I thought my best friend might be happy that I'd finally gotten a guy of my own, but you're being so negative, I can't help wonder if you're not a teeny-weeny bit jealous that I've snagged a cute guy and you're not dating right now."

"That's crazy," I said angrily. "Of course I'm not jealous. I care about you, you dummy! I'm trying to protect you."

"Well, don't," she said firmly. "I don't want protecting. I've been protected for all my life. Maybe I should forget all the rules and start having fun!"

"If that's what you really want . . ." I said helplessly.

"It is," she said. "You just have to trust me, Deb."

"I'll try," I said.

I hung up the phone slowly, trying to ignore the sinking feeling in my stomach. *Maybe he won't even ask her out again, and I'm worrying for nothing,* I thought. *After all, she's not his type. Having her around is bad for his image. He's just being nice to her, I bet. She'll be upset when he doesn't call, and I'll have to comfort her and cheer her up, but then things will be back to normal again.*

I put the phone back on my bedside table and slipped out of bed. The delicious smell of coffee greeted me as I opened my bedroom door and went into the kitchen.

"Good morning, honey," my mother called. "You're up early."

"Hi," I mumbled. "I didn't sleep well, and I—" I broke off as I focused on her. "Wow!" I exclaimed, my eyes opening wide for the first time that morning. "You're all dressed up." She was wearing a tailored black suit and a striped silk blouse, panty hose, and pumps, as well as makeup and a neat hairstyle. Since she had gone back to college, her standard garb had been full skirts or pants, T-shirts, and sandals. Lately she had been getting more and more peasant looking, wearing fringed scarves around her neck and white puffy-sleeved blouses, so this new image was more than a shock.

"Are you going on a job interview or something?" I asked, trying to keep the quiver from my voice. I had begun to think that my mother would never work again. Thoughts of a working mother conjured up pleasing images of money to spare, nights at the movies, a clothing allowance for me. . . .

"I'm applying for an internship for the summer," she said. "I applied for one, but I didn't hear anything and I thought I hadn't gotten it. Yesterday they told me to go and be interviewed."

"Where is it?"

"It's at the *Clarion*," she said.

"The *Clarion*? You'll be working at the newspaper all summer?" I asked, picking up her excitement. "That sounds great. My mom, the news hound! I can see it now: front-page headlines: 'Margaret Leslie Scoops *New York Times*! Uncovers Mafia Headquarters in Quiet Rockley Beach!' "

She flashed me an embarrassed little smile. "I haven't gotten it yet," she said. "Do I look all right? I want to make a good first impression."

"You look terrific," I said. "A real lady executive."

"Not too formal?"

"Just right," I said. "I'd hire you."

She grinned. "Thanks," she said. "I am so nervous. I have all these bad memories of the times before when I applied for jobs and was turned down flat. At least I'm being sent by the college this time. That should make a difference, shouldn't it?"

"Of course," I said. "I bet they'll accept whoever the college sends."

She turned and began pouring coffee. "I hope you're right," she said. "I'd really like this. Imagine working on a newspaper for the summer. This will really show me how much pressure I can handle when I'm ready to get a real job."

"You can handle all sorts of pressure," I said. "After all, you've put up with me for almost seventeen years. You've learned to survive without Dad. I think a newspaper will seem like a piece of cake."

"I hope you're right," she said, nervously gulping her coffee. "Heavens, is that the time? I really should be going. See you later, honey. Wish me luck." She bustled around, grabbing her purse, patting her hair, and leaving me feeling breathless as she went out. My life had undergone so many unlikely changes since my parents split up that I thought nothing would faze me anymore. I'd handled my mother the intellectual, my mother the culture buff, my mother the conservationist. Could I now handle my mother the high-powered newspaperwoman? Wistfully I remembered when she was just my mother, when she baked cookies for me and was the leader of my Brownie troop and made my costumes for school plays. Back in the good old days when Dad treated us to ice cream and my best friend was a shy little girl who stayed home reading books!

Once again I found myself wishing longingly. "If only . . ."

Chapter 7 ────────────────

"*A*nything interesting happen yesterday?" Joe asked when I arrived at the Heartbreak.

"Nothing much. A gang of toughs came in and kidnapped my best friend and almost beat up Howard," I said.

He grinned easily. "That all?" he asked. "Are you sure a few Martians didn't land on the back porch, too?"

"You don't believe me, do you?" I demanded. "That's the trouble with you. You never take anything I say seriously."

"Maybe that's because you don't say much that makes sense," he said. "You don't really expect me to believe that this place was invaded by a gang and that they kidnapped your friend?"

"That's what happened," I said, "believe it or not. Better still, ask Howard. He'll tell you that he was an inch away from being mashed to a pulp by a large fist."

Joe looked at me with that sideways, suspicious

look that he always wore when he wasn't sure of me. He liked to have the upper hand and always got extra cautious when he thought I might be getting the better of him. "Okay, I believe you," he said. "And did you call the police or beat them off single-handed?"

"I didn't need to," I said. "They left with your friend Terry."

"I thought it was your friend they kidnapped."

"Their leader kidnapped my friend. The rest of them went with Terry."

Joe shook his head as if he wanted to get his brains in order. "Let me get this straight," he said. "Their leader kidnapped your friend. Did he lead her out at gunpoint or what?"

"Well, she wasn't exactly kidnapped," I had to admit, realizing that I couldn't string him along any longer. "He drove her home after his caveman buddy got ketchup all over her."

Joe grinned. "You ought to write for the soap operas," he said. "You really had me believing you for a second there."

"I'm really not exaggerating very much," I said. "They really were this tough gang of kids. I was scared they'd break up the place and frighten the customers. And one of them really did lift Howard clear off the ground. They're in a heavy metal rock group called the Road Warriors."

Joe relaxed visibly. "Oh, them," he said. "Old Spike, you mean?"

"You know them?"

"Sure. We were at Harbor High together, only they're a year behind me."

"Not anymore," I said. "They're dropping out, from what I understand."

"They're not bad kids," Joe said. "Nothing dangerous about them. A little wild, maybe, but then, wild is cool—in case you haven't noticed!" He put on a macho, sexy look that made me giggle.

"What's so funny?" he demanded.

"You are," I said.

"Maybe your giggling is just a nervous reaction because you don't want to admit that my wild, untamed body drives you crazy."

I went on giggling. "As a matter of fact," I said, "I've noticed that you've been looking slightly less wild these days. Your hair is shorter, isn't it?"

He put his hand up to his hair, still trying to keep up the cool look while he did so. "Yeah, well, Wendy complained that it hung over my collar and she didn't like that."

"I see," I said. "If Wendy has her way much longer, you'll be coming to work in a three-piece suit and a tie. Oh, and maybe polished, lace-up shoes?"

"Shut up," he said. "Just because Wendy noticed that my hair needed cutting doesn't mean anything. She's right—my hair does have to be short if I'm working around food. So don't go getting things wrong. No girl's going to change the way I am!"

"I'm glad to hear that," I said.

"You are?"

For a second our eyes locked and blazed at each other.

"Sure I am," I said. "At least I know where I stand with you."

"You do?"

"I do," I said. "Your obnoxious and loutish and vain personality is the one thing in the world I can count on."

"Thanks a lot," he said. "You sure know how to give a guy a compliment."

I grinned. "No, I really mean it," I said. "Everyone else keeps changing on me. It's like living in a world of chameleons."

"Your mom's into something else?" he asked.

I nodded. "She's gone off to be Ms. High-powered Newspaperwoman," I said. "And not only that, you remember quiet, studious, shy Pam, my best friend? Well, she's now dating good old Spike from the Road Warriors."

"No!" He looked as if he didn't believe me.

"She went to a movie with him last night, *and* to Uncle Otto's," I said.

"Well, what do you know," he commented. "Maybe there's hope that you'll loosen up one day and start seeing that us ordinary guys are more fun."

"Is that a proposition?" I asked. "Are you suggesting that you'd like to take me to Uncle Otto's? I wonder what Wendy would say to that?"

"I, er, wasn't speaking about us especially," he said quickly, the faintest hint of a blush coming over his face, which in itself was a miracle. "I was just talking about guys like me in general. I was just thinking that the next guy you date should not be an android."

"Don't worry," I said. "I have no intention of dating any more androids. Too boring, for one thing."

"So you don't have your eyes on anyone in particular right now?" he asked, staring hard at me.

"Oh, I don't know about that," I said, trying to look mysterious as I turned away from him. "I kind of liked the look of Spike's friend Danny."

"Danny?" he almost shouted.

"Yes. I don't know," I went on slowly, "there's something about the caveman type that appeals to me. Maybe it's from being around you for so long."

I looked back and grinned.

"Very funny," he said, scowling at me. Then he glanced up at the clock. "What are you standing around for when there is a dishwasher waiting to be unloaded?"

"Oh yes, master," I said sweetly. "I'll get to it right away. Just don't whip me!"

"Get out of here," he said with a grin.

"Which reminds me," I said as I started to stack dishes. "How's your grandfather? Did the doctor say he can start working more hours?"

"Not really," Joe said. "He wants him to keep on taking it easy, at least through the summer."

"Which means we still need an extra person around here," I said. "I wish you'd do something about it, Joe. Put an ad in the paper. We really can't manage with two of us on busy weekends, and I'd like some free time once in a while."

"You're not the only one," he said. "I can't even remember when I had a whole day to myself. This summer is just disappearing, and I haven't even been to the beach. Okay, I'll do something about it, although don't blame me if someone as hopeless as you turns up."

"I think I turned out pretty good in the end," I said.

Joe looked at me slowly. "Maybe not too bad," he said grudgingly. "At least you don't throw hamburgers out the window anymore when you flip them."

"I think I'm pretty darn good," I said. "You should have seen me with all those orders yesterday when Spike was here. I didn't want to leave them alone too long, so I cooked everything in record time."

"Yes, well, you had good training, didn't you?" he said, looking smug. "You learned from one of the world's great experts."

"Oh, shut up," I said. "If they had an ego contest, you'd win hands down."

"Was that fried egos or scrambled egos?" he asked, chuckling to himself as I swept with dignity out of the kitchen.

I got down to serious work then, washing off tables, putting out napkins, filling condiment bottles, and grinning to myself occasionally over our latest exchange. Joe might annoy me from time to time, but at least when I was with him I felt alive— as if life were truly fun and interesting and hopeful. Most of the time these days I didn't feel that way. The future without my father around, without the home I'd grown up in, and now without Grant seemed very scary. Joe kept me going! I glanced back to the kitchen. He had already lit the grill and

I could see the back of his head. His brown curls caught the light just right and his tanned shoulders showed through his muscle shirt.

Maybe Pam wasn't totally wrong about me and Joe, I thought. *Maybe there is a little something there. Maybe even one day . . .* I let my imagination drift into a daydream where I was riding behind Joe on his motorcycle. My hair streamed out in the wind as we rounded the sharp bends along the coast road. Then we parked by a deserted beach and he took my hand to help me across the rocks. Then, when we were all alone beneath the cliffs, we slowly turned toward each other, as we had done before, and his arms came around me. . . .

I was snapped abruptly back to reality by the sound of insistent knocking. Someone was tapping on the locked front door—or rather, hammering now. I glanced at the clock and saw that it was only ten-forty-five. We didn't open until eleven. I put on my most efficient face as I walked toward the door and opened it.

"I'm sorry," I said in my best employee voice, "but we don't open until eleven."

Then I saw that the person outside was Wendy. She didn't look too overjoyed to see me. In fact, she looked me up and down as if I were a worm that had emerged with the last rainstorm.

"Oh, er, hi, Peggy. Is Joe here yet?" she asked, already looking past me as if she were about to mow me down.

"He's in the kitchen," I said, "and my name's Debbie."

"Oh, of course, sorry, Debbie," she said. "I never can remember names."

She began to push in past me. "So Joe's in the kitchen?" she asked sweetly. Without waiting for an answer, she swept through. "Surprise, sweetie," she squealed, then jumped up and down in true cheerleader fashion as he spun around toward her.

"Wendy?" I heard his startled gasp. "What are you doing here?"

She sidled over to him, standing so close to him that she was almost touching. "That doesn't sound as if you're very pleased to see me!" she said.

He looked definitely embarrassed. "Of course I'm pleased to see you," he said. "It's just that I'm in the middle of work."

"I was shopping in those adorable little boutiques down on Beach Row," she said, "and I saw two adorable dresses, but I can't decide which one I like best, so I thought I'd bring you down to help me choose."

He looked at her with that same dangerous wild-animal look he sometimes gave me. "But, Wendy, I'm working," he said. "I just told you. Customers will start arriving in fifteen minutes. I have to get the grill going."

Her gaze swiveled back to me. "I'm sure Peggy can handle things alone for a while," she said. "Can't you, Peggy?"

Joe looked across to me, then back at Wendy. "Her name is Debbie," he said. "You met her the other day, remember?"

"Oh, yes," I said coolly. "We met all right."

"Yes, we met, didn't we, Debbie?" Wendy cooed,

switching on the charm suddenly. "And I'm sure you could spare Joe for a few minutes, couldn't you? Just long enough for me to show him these two adorable dresses?"

"Oh, I don't think so," I said, turning to her with my most serious face. "You see, Joe thinks I'm a pretty hopeless waitress. I throw hamburgers out of windows and things. I don't think he'd trust me alone."

I saw the amusement flicker in Joe's eyes. He was definitely enjoying having two women fighting over him. I saw the pout beginning on Wendy's lips and decided to move in for the kill while I was still ahead.

"Hey, I know what," I said brightly, giving them both a big smile. "Wendy could give us a hand. That way we'd get done quickly, and you could pop out to the store with her, Joe."

Wendy looked at me as if she didn't quite understand what I was saying. "You want me to help you *work*?" she asked.

"Sure," I said. "You could do all the things Joe doesn't trust me to do. You know, like making sure the bathrooms are clean and polishing the french fryer . . ."

She shot him an alarmed look. "I'm not dressed for . . . *work*," she said. "I was in the middle of shopping. I only came down because I wanted to get your opinion on a dress. I wanted the dress you liked me best in, Joe."

"Tell you what," he said quickly, glancing across at me before I could move in for another stab. "You can cut up all this lettuce for me while I get the patties out of the freezer and then I'll come with you. I'll get you an apron, okay?"

"Okay," she said, beaming at him. "Wow, what a lot of lettuce. Are you feeding rabbits or something?"

"It's for the hamburgers," Joe said. "Here, chop it on this board and then put it in this big bowl. Got that?"

"Sure," she said, still dancing around excitedly. "Board then bowl. Got it." She picked up the first head of lettuce. "I think I'll get the hang of this in a jiffy," she said. "It doesn't seem hard at all."

I scowled at her back as I picked up a mop and headed for the bathroom. Had I sounded like that only a few months ago? I had a horrible feeling that I might have come across a little like Wendy. Not as bad, of course, but definitely like a princess trapped in a bad dream.

Joe bumped into me coming out of the bathroom again. "Look, Debbie," he said, almost whispering as he passed me, "I'm sorry about this. I won't stay long. You can handle it, can't you?"

"Do you trust me not to throw the hamburgers out the window?" I asked.

"Of course. Look, I'll make it up to you," he whispered. "It's just that when Wendy gets an idea in her head she can be a bit of a pain. You do understand, don't you?"

"Oh, sure," I said. "It's okay. I understand perfectly. Only make sure you hurry back."

"Why?" he asked with interest. "Will you miss me?"

"No, but she'll make you buy a shirt to match her new dress if you aren't quick," I quipped, and walked past him to join Wendy in the kitchen.

Chapter 8 _____

*I*t was a very busy day at the café. The weather was cloudy and windy, so maybe the beach wasn't inviting, and we had nonstop customers from the moment we opened until late afternoon. Joe had arrived back from his little shopping spree to find me rushing up and down trying to fill ten orders at once.

"I got out of there as quickly as I could," he said as he hurried into his uniform jacket. "She took hours making up her mind. The moment I said I liked one dress, she said she liked the other, but before the girl could ring it up, she said she wasn't sure again." He shook his head. "Are all girls that bad when they're shopping?"

"Some of us never have a chance to go shopping," I said smoothly. "Some of us are working hard, slaving away with dishpan hands, trying to fill in for our colleagues who keep disappearing."

"I think you're enjoying this," he commented as he took some glasses from me and sloshed soda into them. "I also think you enjoyed teasing Wendy."

"She deserved it," I said, setting the first glass none too gently on a tray. "She acted like I was Cinderella and she was one of the ugly stepsisters."

Joe grinned. "I do wish you girls wouldn't keep fighting over me," he said. "Didn't they teach you to share in kindergarten? There's enough of me to go around, you know."

"I was not fighting over you!" I exclaimed with great dignity. "I just didn't enjoy being put down by someone who sweeps in here as if she owns the place."

"My mistake," he said, his eyes teasing. "I got the strong impression that you didn't enjoy seeing Wendy with me."

"Only because she was interrupting our work," I said. "Nothing more than that."

"Sure," he said.

"You don't believe me?"

"I think it was kind of nice that you were prepared to fight for me," he said. "It was good for my ego."

"Your ego doesn't need any help," I said, "and will you stop grinning at me. You just overfilled that glass!"

He tipped soda out of the glass and put it on the tray, which I then carried out to the waiting customers. *Some nerve he's got,* I thought. *He enjoyed two women fighting over him! Wendy's welcome to him. They belong together—they both think too much of themselves.*

"Hey, watch it," a boy at the nearest table growled. "You're spilling my drink over the table."

"Sorry," I muttered. "It was filled too full. I'll clean it up for you."

I tried not to think about Joe and Wendy for the rest of the day.

By late afternoon I was exhausted. When Joe yelled, I thought he was scolding me for sitting at a corner table and having a soda. But he was telling me that my mother was on the phone. She never called me at work. "Is something wrong?" I asked as soon as I picked up the receiver.

"No, nothing. In fact, everything's perfect," she said. "I just called because I got the job and it's going to be super and I've been assigned to work with this guy called Ralph Robertson who is a top journalist and I'm so happy I want us to go out to dinner to celebrate!"

"Wow, that's great, Mom," I said. "I'm so excited for you. See, I told you, pretty soon we'll be seeing 'Margaret Leslie Reports from White House'!"

She laughed, sounding truly happy for the first time in months. "Hardly," she said. "I've spent the whole day being told about computer commands and column inches until my head is swimming. It's a far cry from the old days on the college newspaper when we wrote everything in pencil and had to paste up with rubber cement! I just hope I can handle it!"

"I'm sure you can," I said. "We Leslies are pretty smart, you know."

She laughed again. "So what about dinner tonight?" she asked. "Do you think you can get off early for once? I'd like to make reservations for eight at Maurice's."

"Wow, we really are splurging," I said excitedly. "The only time I've eaten out in ages has been pizza with Dad. And it just so happens that Joe owes me a favor right now. I'll just tell him I'm leaving early. He's done that to me enough times."

"Wonderful," she said. "I'll go ahead and make the reservations then." Then she added lightly, "Oh, and by the way, I mentioned the idea in front of Ralph Robertson and he says he'd like to join us. It seems like a good idea since I'll be working so closely with him. He has been so helpful all day, and he's a very nice man. I hope you don't mind, Debbie?"

"Oh, er, no, of course not. Good idea," I said. But after I put the phone down, I found that I minded very much. It was our celebration dinner, the first we had had in the longest time. Why couldn't she just explain that to Ralph? Even if he was a celebrity by our town's standards and even if he *had* been very nice to her, I still didn't want him at dinner with us.

The moment I saw him, I didn't like him. As soon as he walked across the restaurant, his jacket slung in a studied but casual manner over one shoulder, I knew that he was a jerk. I really don't know why, because he was very nice to me and very nice to Mom, too. Maybe that was the problem: he was almost too good-looking, with those sort of rugged features you usually see in ads for deodorant soaps. His hair was such a perfect blend of black tinged with gray that it must have had some help from a bottle, and his clothes were so well tailored that they must have been handmade and very expensive. In fact, I was sure he must spend most of his salary on his clothes! In many ways Ralph Robertson reminded me of a grown-up version of my ex-boyfriend Grant—someone who obviously thought a lot of himself and his appearance—and instinctively I did not want a grown-up Grant paying attention to my mother!

"So this is little Debbie," he said. His voice had a southern sweetness to it, sticky as molasses. "Your mom's already told me a lot about you." And he flashed me his winning smile.

I was not about to be won. "I'm not so little," I said. "I'm a whole inch taller than my mother."

He laughed and gave Mom an isn't-she-cute-and-adorable look that I found totally annoying.

Mom must have sensed my mood because she coughed nervously. "Er, Mr. Robertson has been so helpful all day. He's been really patient explaining how the computers work and all the procedures. I'd have been completely lost without him."

He smiled at her. "Nonsense, ma'am, if you'll pardon me for contradicting you," he said heartily. "You're a very quick study. You got everything right away. And please, call me Ralph, because I'd like to call you Margaret."

My mother blushed prettily. "It's fine with me . . . Ralph," she answered.

"Wonderful," he went on heartily. "You know, I feel that I've known you much longer than one day. In fact, I have the strangest feeling of déjà vu as I look at you. Is it possible that we met before somewhere, very long ago when we were silly, carefree students, maybe?"

I looked from one to the other, like a spectator at a tennis match. *How can she be falling for this stuff?* I asked myself angrily. *He's so phony, anyone could see through him.*

"She was never a silly, carefree student until a couple of months ago," I said bluntly. "When she was last at college, she was married to my dad. Maybe she reminds you of someone else!"

He looked at me, his cold blue eyes displaying the slightest flicker of annoyance before he smiled again. "I can see where you get your intelligence," he said. "You're as sharp as your mother."

"Sometimes too sharp," my mother said, giving me a look that clearly said, *You'd better watch it, young woman.*

For the rest of the meal, my mother looked impressed and excited as Ralph told us about all his newspaper scoops and award-winning articles. Every time he made one of his corny remarks and she smiled up at him, I started to giggle. I couldn't help myself. I kept picking up my glass of water and sipping it whenever I felt a giggle coming on, and twice the giggle made the water go down the wrong way and I ended up choking and making my mother glare at me even harder.

"I don't know what your problem was tonight," she said in an icy tone as we drove home, "but you were behaving very strangely."

"It was Mr. Robertson," I said. "He brought out the worst in me, I guess."

"I don't know why," she said. "I thought he was quite charming."

"So did Little Red Riding Hood when she first met the wolf," I commented.

She gave me a sharp look. "I think you're being very juvenile about this," she said.

"Me, juvenile?" I asked. "Oh, come on, Mom, you were giggling like a little schoolgirl every time he said anything to you. You fell for all those corny lines he dished out."

"What corny lines?" she demanded. "Just because Mr. Robertson found me attractive and is old-fashioned enough to know how to pay a compliment—"

"About the cornflowers at the table matching your eyes?" I asked, trying to suppress another giggle.

"I don't see anything wrong with that," she said. "Just plain old-fashioned southern courtesy. He's from Georgia, you know."

"Either that or he's seen *Gone With the Wind* too many times," I said.

She swung the car into our parking lot, none too gently. "I think you're going to have to get used to the fact that there will be men in my life sometimes," she said. "I'm still a young woman. I don't intend to sit around pining for your father for the rest of my life."

"At least you could give him time," I blurted out. "If you gave him a year on his own, I bet he'd realize he can't make it without you and he'd come back. I bet he misses you already. He almost says so when we have lunch together. He always asks about you."

"Maybe I don't want him back," she said slowly.

"You don't want him back?" I asked. I was so shocked, it came out as a squeak. "You don't want to get back together with Dad?"

"I'm not sure," she said. "He's put me through a lot of suffering. I don't know if I'd be prepared to forget that. I don't even know if I'd want to start from square one with him. It might be easier to make a fresh start with a new man." She brought the car to an abrupt halt and turned off the engine. "Besides," she said, "it isn't likely to happen, so it's useless talking about it."

I stared at her in horror. It was as if someone who looked like my mother, with my mother's voice, had suddenly peeled off her skin and revealed herself to be one of the Lizard People. I'd always thought she worshiped my father and would do anything to get him back. And secretly, in my heart of hearts, I'd always believed that they would get back together again, if only I could wait patiently until they missed each other enough. Now it didn't seem as though it would happen, after all. I'd be stuck for the rest of my days as a mixed-up child from a broken home!

I felt strangely cold as I climbed into bed that night. I kept thinking of my mother with Ralph Robertson.

Maybe I'm reading too much into this, I told myself as I curled into a tight little ball. *She invited the guy to dinner with us because she's working with him. That doesn't mean she's going to marry him or anything. Maybe she did see through his terrible corny lines but she was flattered anyway to have a guy paying attention to her again. I bet he's just an old smoothie who turns on the charm for all the women he meets and he's not interested in Mom at all. I bet I'm doing all this worrying for nothing.*

But after a week in which my mother had fallen for a slick dandy with a smooth line and Pam had started dating a hot-rodding rock singer, I had a hard time convincing myself that anything in the world was going to make sense again.

Chapter 9 _____

On Sunday I actually had a whole day all to myself. Joe's grandfather had announced that he wanted to get back into the swing of working, so Joe had kindly told me I could take a day off. "Don't worry, we can handle it," he said. "Besides, Wendy was threatening to stop by; I'll put her to work if we need an extra hand."

"I bet she throws hamburgers out the windows," I said.

"Well, if you want to come in to keep an eye on her, you're welcome to," he said quickly. "I enjoyed your last little battle."

"That's okay," I answered. "I think I'll just take my day off. Who knows when I'll get another one."

So I woke up on Sunday morning to a brilliant blue sky and the rare treat of knowing that I wouldn't have to do a thing all day. I made coffee and took a cup in to my mother.

"It's a beautiful day," I said, opening the curtains. "I've got a great idea—let's go on a picnic somewhere."

She sat up and took a sip of the coffee. "Oh, honey, I'd have loved to," she said, "but Ralph's taking me out to lunch."

"Ralph Robertson? The creep?"

"He's not a creep," she said. "He's actually a very pleasant man."

I started to walk toward the door. "I didn't think you'd be so desperate that you'd run after the first guy who paid any attention to you," I said. "You could do a lot better, you know."

The color flooded her cheeks. "I am not running after him, Deborah," she said. "He's just reciprocating for our dinner last week. He told me about this little seafood restaurant, and when I said I hadn't ever been there, he invited me. Simple as that."

"I see," I said.

She swung her legs over the side of the bed and reached for her robe. "I don't see why you dislike him so much."

"Because he's a smooth-talking creep," I said. "I bet he makes a pass at every new woman who comes to work there."

She looked at me frostily. "I've simply agreed to have lunch with him," she said. "You're making it sound like a weekend in Las Vegas!"

"I just don't want to see you waste your time with a phony," I said. "Ralph Robertson acts charming, but I'll bet the only person he really thinks about is himself. He's just too smooth to be real!"

"Don't worry about me, I'm a big girl. I can take care of myself," she said, and finally smiled at me. "I'm just going to eat seafood and then come home again, okay, Grandma?"

"Okay," I said, laughing. "But make sure you're home early. I don't trust that Ralph Robertson alone with you after dark."

She laughed, too. "You're lucky I never gave you such a bad time with Grant," she said.

"I was always sensible, and you knew it," I said smugly. "Besides, Grant always acted like a Boy Scout. Nobody had to worry about Grant."

Then I reminded myself that at that moment he was up at his family's cabin on the lake with another girl, and I was alone in a crummy condo. I went back to my room and called Pam for some cheering up.

"Guess what?" I asked her. "I've got a whole long, beautiful day off. Do you think your family will let you out of grandmother duty and we can go somewhere? There's an art festival down at Whitney Cove. We could stop by my dad's place for dinner maybe."

She hesitated for a moment before saying, "I'd love to, Deb, but I promised Spike I'd come and watch him play."

"You're seeing Spike again?"

She giggled. "Isn't it wonderful?" she said. "Did you ever believe that something like this would happen to me?"

"Never in a million years," I said. "What do you see in him, Pam?"

"I see a great-looking guy who drives great cars

and who for some reason thinks I'm special," she said breathlessly. "And that's good enough for me."

"But, Pam," I began, before she cut me off.

"What's with you anyway? Since when did they appoint you god of who is right for me? You've only had one boyfriend yourself, and I didn't go around acting surprised that he noticed you or telling you how wrong he was!"

"There's a slight difference between Grant and Spike," I said, thrown off balance by Pam's anger. "Nobody ever worried when I went out with Grant. He was safe and reliable."

"Maybe I don't want safe and reliable," she said. "You should be happy that I'm happy."

"I am happy for you, Pam," I said, because I could hear myself sounding like an old grouch when my best friend was clearly flying three feet above the ground, "but you will be careful, won't you?"

"Sometimes it's fun not to be careful," she said. "Like on Friday night—we were pulled over for speeding and Spike talked his way out of it. You should have heard him. It was so much fun."

"You think that was *fun*?"

"Sure. Why not? Sixteen years of being good old reliable Pam is enough."

"But that's the way you are, Pam. You don't really belong with someone like Spike."

"Just don't try to run my life for me, okay?" she said. "I don't want to talk to you if you're only going to lecture me all the time, Debbie."

I said good-bye and hung up. What had happened to the world? My mother was all breathless about a date with Ralph the Creep, and Pam didn't even sound like herself anymore.

"What a great summer this has turned out to be," I said to myself as I walked alone down the beach later that day. I had decided not to drive to Whitney Cove. It just didn't sound fun to go by myself. So instead I went to the first deserted beach I could find and walked along the water's edge. I stomped at the sand savagely, watching it rise in satisfying puffs behind me. I felt scared and angry and confused and, for once, I had nobody to talk to about it. I thought about my phone conversation with Pam and realized that I was in danger of losing my best friend. Was I trying to run her life for her? I wondered. No, it was just that I could see Spike for who he truly was, I defended myself. Although I guess I did come across as the Ann Landers of the teenage set.

But if I saw her driving a car toward the edge of a cliff, I'd try to warn her, I argued with myself again. Someone like Spike only meant trouble in the long run. I would have to keep my mouth shut and just pray that she came to her senses. . . .

"Everyone in the world has gone bananas except me," I muttered to myself. "It's one of Howard's horror movies come to life. Body snatchers have taken over my family and friends!" I could see it all: Pam would end up as Mrs. Spike and get married in a leather veil with studs on it, and my mother would marry Ralph the Creep and go to live in a mansion and put magnolia blossoms in her hair and keep saying, "Well, I do declare" while she fanned herself. Ralph would probably hire me as a slave for the cotton plantation! I let my imagination drift and saw my mother, in a long flowery dress and big hat, sipping lemonade on the porch while Ralph strode around cracking his whip and snarling, "Get working, slaves." I'd pick cotton until my hands were raw, then stagger home, weak from exhaustion, to a little shack on the bayou. I saw myself eating collard greens (whatever they were) while outside a guitar was strumming and everyone was singing "Nobody Knows the Trouble I've Seen"! Then I stopped to giggle. This was going a bit far, even for my dramatic imagination.

"She won't marry Ralph Robertson. She can't marry Ralph Robertson," I murmured. "She's just flattered right now. She'll see through him soon enough, and then things will be back to normal."

But when I got home, she was lying with her feet up on the sofa, fanning herself with *TV Guide*, a dreamy, faraway look on her face.

"We had a lovely lunch," she said. "I haven't had lobster in ages. It tasted so good and Ralph was such good company. He's such an amusing man and has so many wonderful stories."

"About life on the plantation?"

"What?"

"Nothing."

She smiled. "We sat there for three hours and just talked. The time just slipped away. . . ."

"That's great, Mom," I muttered.

"How was your day?" she asked. "Did you go to that art festival and visit your father?"

"No, I decided not to," I answered. "I didn't feel like company."

"You need to find yourself a new boyfriend," she said. "You have hardly been out since you broke up with Grant."

"I don't exactly get a lot of time to meet guys, stuck at the café all the time," I said. "And I'd hardly want to date the guys I meet down there."

She looked concerned. "Maybe we can afford to get you a country-club membership for the summer. Maybe they'd give me a special rate just for you. Then you could be around all your old friends."

For a second a picture flashed across my mind of the good old days last summer, of me lounging around the pool with my friends, talking and laughing, having barbecues and tennis games. I barely managed to stop myself from blurting out that I'd like to join again.

"Thanks, Mom, but it wouldn't work," I said. "I don't belong there anymore. I'd only feel like an outsider. I'd better just stick to working and saving money this summer."

"You need some fun, too," she reminded me.

"I know," I said, "but I'm not quite sure where to find it anymore. I'm sort of floating in a vacuum right now. It will be better when I'm back at school and there are plays and clubs and things—if I ever get time to join them, that is."

"We'll make time," she said. "I'm earning some money this summer. That should at least make things a little easier in the fall for both of us."

"You'll probably have married Ralphie and be living in a southern mansion by then," I said before I thought about it.

She laughed. "Whatever gave you that idea?" she asked. "You and your imagination." But I noticed that she also blushed.

When I arrived at the Heartbreak the next morning, Joe was there ahead of me.

"Did you survive without me yesterday?" I asked.

"Oh, yes, everything was fine," he said. "My grandfather did some cooking for a while, and Wendy stopped by and helped out. It went just great, actually."

"That's good," I said, and started to take off my jacket.

"And by the way," he went on casually, "our worries are over. You know how you kept going on about finding an extra person to help out?"

I looked up excitedly. "You've found us a new waitress? When does she start?"

"Today," he said.

"Is she experienced?"

"Very," he said, and grinned. "I know you're going to love this—her name is Wendy."

"*Wendy?*" I shrieked. "*The* Wendy? Wendy with all the teeth and hair? Wendy's going to be working here?"

He grinned sheepishly. "Somehow I didn't think you'd be too thrilled."

"Thrilled?" I went on yelling. "You must be out of your mind. That girl's got you tied around her little finger."

His eyes flashed as they always did when he was being attacked. "Hey, you were the one who kept on nagging me about finding extra help. Well, I found it, so quit beefing."

"We need someone to help us around here," I snapped. "She doesn't know a thing about waitressing."

"She helped out yesterday," Joe said. "She thought it was fun and she's saving up for a new car, so it should work out pretty well."

"Oh, great," I said sarcastically. "Just great. Peachy keen, in fact."

He came over to me and stood close enough that I couldn't move without bumping into him. "Look, Debbie,' he said quietly, "Wendy's really a nice girl. You'll like her once you get to know her, and you did say you needed extra help, so let's give her a try, okay?"

"Sure," I said unsteadily. "What do I have to say about it, anyway? I'm just the hired help. You're the boss."

"I'm glad you've finally admitted it," he quipped, but for once I couldn't think of a smart answer.

I turned away and began working furiously at loading the napkin holders. My stupid pride would not let me say what was in my heart. I wanted to beg him not to hire her, to tell him that nothing would be the same at the Heartbreak if she came to work there. I had spent the last few months telling myself that I couldn't stand Joe Garbarini, that he was everything I despised in a boy, and that all I enjoyed doing with him was fighting. Now I knew that wasn't true. He might have been the exact opposite of any boy I'd ever had a crush on before, but I didn't want to share him with Wendy; I wanted him all to myself.

Chapter 10 —————————

Wendy came to work at the Heartbreak and a big cloud of gloom settled over me. I'm not normally a gloomy person, but it seemed that this summer everything was conspiring against me. I wished over and over that I had not kept bugging Joe about finding another waitress. In fact, I'd willingly have slaved twelve hours a day to have things back the way they were. The moment Wendy walked in, nothing was the same. To begin with, she was supposed to be helping, but she only wanted to do the fun things.

"I just can't get the hang of this fryer," she complained to Joe, gazing at him helplessly. "How about if I decorate the burgers for you instead. I'm good at that. See how artistic this looks with the tomato slices like this? Just like a commercial, right?"

So Wendy got to hang around, waiting for burgers to decorate, and I got to stand over the fryer, wiping the splatters of oil off it, scooping out a steady stream of fries.

The second day she broke a fingernail. "Just look at this, Joe," she complained. "Do you know how long it's taken me to grow these? All this scrubbing and cleaning is just wrecking my hands. Why doesn't Debbie finish off the sink, and I'll go wait tables?"

"It's kind of busy out there," I said. "Do you think you can handle it?"

She looked at me with those innocent blue eyes and that smile that somehow didn't go beyond her lips. "What can be so hard about burger and fries, fries and burger?" she said sweetly. "I've learned a million cheerleading routines. I'm sure I can handle a few little food orders."

I glanced over at Joe, but he had deliberately turned his back and was loading glasses into the dishwasher. I made up orders and handed them to her, secretly praying that she would drop them all down someone's neck. But she made it to the tables okay and appeared a few minutes later.

"You got things mixed up, Debbie," she said, still very sweetly. "You had the fries on the order with two cheeseburgers and you put onions on the hot dog when I said no onions. Try to concentrate next time, all right?"

"I made up the orders like you told me," I said, fighting to keep my cool. "Maybe in the future you should take the pad and write them down so we agree."

"I don't mind that if it would help you, Debbie," she said, giving me her fake smile.

Next day Wendy came in wearing bright orange rubber gloves. "I just have to think of my hands if I'm going to get any modeling work this summer," she said. She carried out orders still wearing the gloves.

"Hey, that reminds me, did anyone see that movie on TV last night?" I heard Howard ask as she placed the orders on the table. "Great movie, about this creature from a volcano with bright red skin who comes down to this village during an eruption and goes around killing people?"

"Euww, Howard, you're being gross again," Ashley complained.

"It was just like those gloves," Howard explained. "Her hands look just like the monster in the movie. His hands looked just like that, and you kept seeing them coming in through windows and—"

"I don't think I want these fries now," Ashley said, pushing her plate away. I peeked out of the kitchen and noticed that one girl at the next table was frozen with a ketchup-drenched fry poised in midair and a look of total nausea on her face.

"You've got to make Wendy stop using those gloves to serve the customers," I muttered to Joe. "She's grossing everyone out. Howard was saying how she looked like a monster in a movie on TV."

Joe looked up and grinned, meeting my gaze. "I can't stop her waiting tables," he said, "or I'll be paying her just for putting tomatoes on burgers."

"Then tell her it isn't working out," I pleaded. "Tell her she's just not cut out for waitressing."

"She reminds me of you when you first started here," he said.

"She does not. I was not a total flake!" I said. "I did my share of the work, and I didn't make a fuss all the time, *and* I didn't try to blame my mistakes on other people."

Wendy came in as I was finishing my sentence. She looked from me to Joe and back again. "Someone was complaining the french fries were burned, Debbie," she said. "I guess you weren't keeping an eye on the timer." Her look said very clearly: *You were talking to Joe behind my back and I don't like it.*

"Gee, I'm sorry," I said. "I didn't realize you were an expert on french-fry temperatures as well as cheerleading."

Her lips began to form the famous pout. "Joe-Joe," she said sweetly, "let's get out of here and go to lunch somewhere? I really need some fresh air and some food that isn't greasy. Come with me?"

"Wendy, we have a café to run," Joe said.

"It's pretty empty right now. Only those creepy kids in the back," she said, peering through the doorway. "That little nerdy one was telling the most disgusting story. I don't know why you let them sit here for hours and hardly buy anything. I'd throw them out."

"They like it here," Joe said, "and they are our regular customers. They pay the rent, Wendy."

"But they're so gross," Wendy said. "That awful little nerd with the hair that stands on end and that girl with all the hair. Where do people like that come from?"

"Ashley goes to your school, doesn't she?" I said, unable to resist. "She seemed to know you."

Wendy's dainty nose crinkled. "Everybody knows me," she said, "but I don't exactly hang around with her, uh, type. I mean, does someone make her dress that way? She probably scares people away from the café."

She made no attempt to keep her voice down, and I saw Ashley glance up and then look away.

"Cool it, Wendy," Joe said, and he went back to work at the grill.

I found myself feeling angrier by the minute about how Wendy had put Ashley and Howard down. "Ashley's really very nice," I said. "She just dresses funny. They're all very nice."

Wendy smiled at me, sort of like a tiger would probably smile if a person walked into his den at dinnertime. "You're such a sweet person, Debbie," she said, "but I guess it's easier for you. You fit in here and I don't."

I almost had to smile myself, since it was not that long before that everyone at the Heartbreak would have agreed that I stood out like a sore thumb. The realization that I now fit in sent a warm glow through me. It was nice to be considered the insider when Wendy was not.

"Then why don't you leave?" I asked. "I'm sure you could find a job with your sort of people."

"So that you could get your hands on Joe?" she asked. "Although I wouldn't bother if I were you, you're not his type."

"Don't worry," I said. "I'm not even interested."

"Sure," she said with a grin. She walked over to Joe and slipped her arm around his waist, whispering something into his ear. I watched him gaze down at her with that silly smile on his face. How could he be so dumb? I wondered angrily. How could he let her get away with things and not see what a phony she was? How could he let her boss him around?

A few minutes later he told me that he and Wendy were popping out for a few minutes.

"And you want me to do *all* the work while you're gone?" I asked. "What is it this time, new shoes? New fingernails? Matching his-and-her socks?"

He grinned, then remembered that Wendy was right there. "She just needs to get out for a while," he said. "She's never worked before and she's finding it kind of hard."

I spluttered. "She still hasn't worked," I said. "Two days here and the most stressful thing she has done is choose the right size tomato for the bun!"

"It took you a while, too," he said. "You found it difficult here to begin with."

"I didn't notice you walking me around the block to calm me down," I commented bitterly.

"You didn't want me to," he said, and turned away abruptly. "You made it very clear that you didn't want me anywhere near you."

Which was true, of course. I tried to tell myself that I had not wanted anything from Joe Garbarini.

I had always fought with him and told him to get lost.

I only liked the mental exercise of our little fights, with their occasional hint of flirtation, but nothing more. If anyone had asked me, I'd have told them that Joe's teasing annoyed me most of the time, that I found it hard to put up with constant macho statements. So it really should not have bothered me at all to see him with Wendy. I should have been happy that she was taking up his time and letting me get on with my work in peace. I should have been really happy that he wasn't around to bug me constantly—

But I wasn't. I found having no time alone with Joe the hardest thing of all to bear. Which surprised even me. I hadn't realized before how very much I looked forward to our little fights, our constant sparring and teasing. Now that Wendy was always around, we didn't fight anymore. In fact, Joe hardly said a thing to me except to tell me what needed doing. If we ever did begin a conversation, Wendy miraculously appeared out of thin air and slipped an arm through Joe's or immediately needed help with something at the other end of the café.

At the end of the first week Wendy came into the bathroom when I was changing out of my uniform. "Debbie, I've been meaning to talk to you," she said. "You know Joe's grandfather can't afford to have us both working full-time. Joe says you wanted more time off anyway. He says that he and his grandfather can spell each other and we'll have to work out a schedule between ourselves. So maybe you'd like to let me know when you want to work. I thought maybe I'd do days and you could do evenings, if that's all right. I mean, you don't have anything to do with your evenings right now, do you?"

I didn't say anything, but the same confused and scared feelings came rushing back as I drove home. Was this the beginning of the end? Would Wendy succeed in getting rid of me?

Come on, be fair, I tried to tell myself. *You've been begging for more time off, complaining that you never have days to yourself. Now you're offered them and you're upset!*

I knew that was the reasonable approach, but inside my head a little voice kept whispering, *What if there is no more Heartbreak? Where would you go then? What would you do? You'd have nowhere and nobody anymore.*

"What's the matter, sweetheart?" my mother asked as I came in and dumped my purse down on the counter with a loud thump. "You look really down in the dumps."

"Joe's girlfriend has come to work at the café, and she's ruining everything," I said, coming over to sit on the arm of the sofa where Mom was sitting with a pile of papers.

"Joe's the young man with the motorcycle and the hair, right?"

"Not the hair anymore," I said. "Wendy made him get it cut."

"And she's giving him a hard time."

"You can say that again," I muttered. "She does almost no work, she bosses me around, and if I dare to talk to Joe she always calls him away. It's no fun down there anymore."

My mother nodded, then said, "If you're so unhappy, why don't you quit and find another job? You don't have to stay in a job that's not fun."

"I guess so," I said. "She even told me tonight that I'd have less hours to work because she was there."

"Honey, there are plenty of good jobs around," my mother said. "You could always get a waitressing job somewhere else. After all, you're experienced now. You could go somewhere elegant and get big tips!"

"I know," I said with a sigh, "but it wouldn't be the same. I know all the customers down at the Heartbreak, Mom. I feel like I belong there."

"So you don't want to quit?"

"No!" I said.

"Then don't let this Wendy push you around," my mother said. "Fight for your rights. I wish I had learned to earlier in my life. I'm not used to fighting and as a result people walk all over me."

"At the newspaper?" I asked.

Her face softened. "Oh, no," she said. "Ralph is being so sweet. He's letting me take my time getting into the swing of things, and he's really patient. He lets me help him on stories, too. I'm having a great time there." She broke off suddenly, her eyes lighting up. "Hey, I've just had an idea," she said. "You could come and help me at the newspaper. I've got a lot of facts to gather for a big article. I'm sure Ralph wouldn't mind."

For a second there it sounded like a good idea.

I pictured myself with a pencil behind my ear, looking up from a big law book and saying, "I've found just what we need. We can stop them from putting through that freeway forever!" Then I pictured Ralph standing there beside my mother telling her that her eyes were as green as computer screens or something equally nauseating.

"I don't know, Mom," I said. "Thanks for the offer, but I don't think so."

"How about if you come down and visit tomorrow," she said. "I need to be picked up anyway because my car has to go in for that tune-up, remember? I'll show you around, and you can at least see what a newspaper office looks like."

"I'd like that," I said. "I'd like to see the great Margaret Leslie in action!"

She laughed. "Not so great, yet," she said. "They have you start off doing things like filing and making the coffee. Ralph's being very nice to me by letting me do this research. Some of the other interns haven't gotten beyond the gofer stage yet."

"I bet the other interns don't have your talent," I said.

"You know, I think I might just have some talent," she said thoughtfully. "I'm finding some fascinating facts for this article, things that have really made me think."

"Then I'll have to come and see you in action," I said. "What time do you want me to pick you up?"

"If you come about an hour early, I'll show you around," she said. "But one thing . . ."

"Which is?"

"Please try to be polite to Ralph," she said. "I'm the new girl on the block at the newspaper, and I don't want a replay of your rudeness the other night."

"Don't worry, Mom," I said. "I'll behave myself. I'll be a model daughter in front of Ralph." *It won't be easy, though,* I added to myself.

Chapter 11 _____

*T*oward the end of the day I drove over to the *Clarion*, went up to the main newsroom, and made my way over to my mother's desk. She was peering at her computer screen and frowning in concentration. "It keeps saying *Bad Command*," she muttered, not looking up. "Why are my commands bad? Do you think it doesn't like me?"

"Don't ask me," I said. "I don't even know what computer system you use here."

She looked up and saw it was me. "Oh, Debbie, it's you. I thought you were Ralph," she said. So, the cute remark about the computer not liking her was aimed at him!

"I'm done for the day, so I can give you a quick tour," she said, looking around. "Just let me get out of this mess and file these notes. Maybe Ralph can do it for me." I looked up to see him coming toward her, his jacket slung over one shoulder again. Maybe the guy had no left shoulder. Or maybe he had a hump like Quasimodo and always carried his jacket to hide it, I thought, and had to look away to hide my grin.

"Got a problem, Margaret?" he asked, coming to stand behind her chair.

"It keeps telling me I've given a bad command," she said, looking up at him with a dumb helpless look. "Do you think maybe it doesn't like me or something?"

So she got to use her line, after all. It obviously worked, too, because he rested his hand on the back of her chair and leaned over, very close to her. "It just doesn't know you yet," he murmured in his deep, rumbling voice. "When it gets to know you, I'm sure it will like you a lot."

I had a sudden urge to make gagging noises like Pam and I used to do when we were younger and watched romantic movies. How can she not see through him? I wondered in amazement. I'd always thought of my mother as a completely practical person.

"There," he was saying. "You were telling it file when you meant save. No problem." He scanned the screen. "You got a lot accomplished today. These notes will be very useful for the feature, Margaret. I'll have to find a way to thank you." He continued to lean across her chair even though the notes were already saved and he didn't need to touch the computer anymore.

I couldn't stand it another minute. "Mom," I said. "If you want to give me a tour, it'll have to be quick or I'll be late for work."

"Work?" Ralph asked. "You have to work in the evenings? What's your mother trying to do to you, keep you out of trouble?" He laughed at his own joke.

"I have to support myself," I said coldly. "I have to pay my car expenses and save for college."

Ralph nodded enthusiastically. "All young people should work," he said. "Prepares them for the real world. I did all sorts of jobs to put myself through college—worked as a lumberjack, on a riverboat, as a farm laborer. They sure as heck made a man out of me."

"I wonder if waitressing will make a man out of me?" I asked before I could stop myself. I saw my mother's frown.

"Well, Debbie, why don't we do that tour?" she said quickly. "And remind me we have to pick up food on the way home," she added, giving me a very clear you-promised-to-behave-yourself look. "What do you want for dinner?"

"I'll be at work," I said. "Just pick up something for yourself."

"I make a very fine fettuccini," Ralph said. "I'll volunteer my services as chef if you'd like."

"We both hate fettuccini," I said before Mom could answer.

"No we don't," she said quickly, "and anyway, you'll be out." She turned to gaze up at him. "I'd love it if you'd come and cook fettuccini, Ralph," she said. "Maybe you can teach me. I've always been a total dunce at pasta."

"There's nothing to it. Just takes the right touch," he said. "All a question of cooking it just until it's al dente, and then adding the right amount of basil."

"I think I'll forget about the tour tonight. I really have to get to work on time," I said, and fled. I knew I was being rude and childish, but I couldn't stop myself.

I worked all evening at the café. When I got home, Ralph's car was still in front of our building.

"I guess it was a long fettuccini lesson," I said, bursting in and watching them scramble to move apart on the sofa.

"The fettuccini was delicious," my mother said hastily. "Ralph is really a good cook. I'll have to make his recipe for you sometime."

"I do have a way with pasta, if I say so myself," Ralph said with a modest smile. "I have a great lasagna recipe, too, Margaret. Perhaps I could make it for you sometime . . . maybe over at my place."

The next evening when I arrived home from the Heartbreak, Ralph's car was there again.

"What happened? Wasn't the stove over at your place working?" I asked before they could greet me.

"Ralph's been having problems with his plumbing," my mother said. "His sink keeps backing up. He's waiting to have it fixed."

"Oh, too bad," I said, deliberately perching myself on the back of the sofa behind them. "What's on TV?" I asked. "Isn't that movie we wanted to watch on tonight—you know, the one where the girl is possessed by the devil and murders her mom's new husband?"

I reached for the remote, but my mother slapped my hand away. "Not now, Debbie, we're talking."

I slid onto the sofa beside them. "Great," I said, "what are we talking about? I love to talk."

"Aren't you tired after all that hard work at the café?" Ralph asked.

"Tired? No, I'm just fine. Ready to go on for hours and hours," I said. "But don't let me interrupt your conversation. Please, go ahead."

Ralph got to his feet. "I really should be going, Margaret," he said. "Got a busy day ahead tomorrow. We want to get that asbestos feature finished. I think we've got some award-winning material there."

"Yes, I think it will make a very powerful exposé," my mother agreed.

"Why don't you walk me to my car," Ralph said, glancing back at me.

"All right," she said.

They went out and I started to load dishes into the dishwasher. I needed to do something because I was feeling guilty about my behavior. I knew I'd acted like a horrible brat, but I couldn't bear to watch my mother making such a fool of herself. I'd almost finished in the kitchen when she came back in. The way she slammed the front door made me look up.

"There," she said. "I hope you are satisfied."

"What do you mean?" I asked warily.

"Ralph has just told me that he doesn't see any future in our relationship. He says he'd like to get to know me better, but he's not sure he can deal with dating a woman with a kid." She paused and stared at me, making me feel uneasy. "I still can't get over you. You even promised just yesterday that you'd behave around him."

"At the office," I said. "The promise didn't extend to after hours. Besides, you really should be grateful to me for getting you off the hook with him."

"I beg your pardon?" my mother asked, enunciating each word.

"You should thank me for saving you from that boring, pompous creep. Did he spend the evening telling you about all the brilliant articles he's written, all the awards he's won, and all the pasta he has cooked?"

"I didn't happen to find him boring or pompous," she said. "I found him charming."

"Oh, Mom, get real," I said with a sigh. "The guy is a pretentious idiot. He talks about himself and how great he is all the time. You deserve better than that."

"Did it ever occur to you that I might not meet anyone better than that?" she asked, and her voice wobbled like a little kid's. "Did it ever occur to you that this might be my one chance for happiness, and that you blew it for me?"

"Oh, come on, Mom," I said, embarrassed, "happiness with Ralph? What would be fun about staying with him, except that you'd never have to cook fettuccini again?"

"What makes you the expert on who is right for me?" she demanded. "You seem to think you know better than I do about what sort of life I should be leading. Every time I join a group or come home with a friend, you immediately tell me what's wrong with them."

"That's because I can see these things clearly and you can't," I said. "And I can see that you don't want to spend the rest of your life being told how to cook fettuccini!"

My mother's face was bright red by now. "You think this is a big joke, don't you?" she suddenly exploded. "You don't think this matters to me at all. Well, it does matter. I'm not a little kid, Deborah. I'm nearly forty years old, and I don't want to be alone for the rest of my life. I didn't ask your father to walk out on me, but now that he has, I don't want to look forward to a lonely old age."

"I understand that, Mom," I said, "but you're not desperate enough to need someone like Ralph Robertson, at least not yet. You're still good-looking. And you're smart and quick. I bet you'll meet loads of guys who will all be better than stupid old Ralph Robertson."

"Maybe," she said. "Maybe I wouldn't have considered marrying him, but I haven't dated in twenty years. I need practice just being around men. If you're going to scare off any man I meet, I'll never get the chance."

She walked past me into the kitchen and began putting the last few items into the dishwasher, creating an awful racket.

I stood there in the doorway as if turned to stone. For the first time I began to realize what I had done. I had deliberately tried to scare off Ralph Robertson because I could see that he was not good enough for her. I had thought I knew better than she did, just as she had said.

What if someone did that to me? I found myself thinking. *What if my mother came down to the café and said that I couldn't work there any more because Joe wasn't a suitable companion for me?* That's what she probably would have thought when she first met him, and I would have been so mad if she'd tried to stop me from going there.

I watched her working, trying to see her as a person, as not just my mother, but a woman who wanted friends and dates, just like me.

I didn't have a guy of my own right now, someone to tell me I was special. I could understand that she wanted the same things I did. I walked up behind her and put a hand awkwardly on her shoulder. "I'm sorry, Mom, really I am," I said. "I guess I did behave like a little kid. I think I was thinking more about me than about you. In some ways I'm not ready for you to start dating yet. I haven't even learned to let go of my father. I didn't want to wreck your life, honest."

She reached up and covered my hand with her own. "It's all right, honey," she said in a tired voice. "And you may be right. Maybe Ralph does make a pass at all the new women who come to work at the *Clarion*. But he made me feel pretty and interesting again. I really needed someone like him to let me know that I could make it in the real world."

"If you like, I'll go talk to him tomorrow," I said. "Tell him I made a mistake. I could say I thought he was someone else, an old ax murderer we used to know. Or that I have schizophrenic fits and I'm really two people, one of whom is scared of men, and I didn't know what I was saying. I'll promise to keep out of his way—you can lock me in the laundry room when he comes over, okay?"

My mother finally laughed. "I should have locked you in the laundry room years ago," she said, "except that that wouldn't have been a punishment for you. Remember how you loved to watch the clothes go around and around? Oh, and remember how I stopped you from putting the cat in just in time?"

I laughed. "I remember," I said. "I thought he'd like it," I said, "and I wanted to see him go around." I turned toward her. "I guess I've always been a little brat, right?"

She smiled. "Most of the time you're pretty okay," she said.

"I'm sure you'll thank me in the long run that you didn't marry Ralph and go to live on the plantation," I said.

She shook her head, still smiling. "I don't know. I really don't know, Debbie," she said. "I might have found him a bit much after a while. He does like to tell me how to do things. Perhaps that would start to get on my nerves."

"And all those clichés," I added. " 'Your eyes as blue as the cornflowers on the table.' I'm surprised the guy doesn't write for a soap opera."

She toyed with a coffee cup, turning it around on the saucer. "As a matter of fact, it was rather nice to be told my eyes were as blue as cornflowers. I don't care if it was a cliché . . . I sort of liked it."

I played with the refrigerator door while I watched her. "I said I was sorry," I muttered, "and I'm beginning to feel worse and worse. I will go and talk to him, Mom. I'll make him come back—"

She put down the cup and grabbed my shoulders. "Forget about Ralph," she said, beginning to laugh. "You know, I really should have given your father custody of you so I'd have some peace and quiet."

"He wouldn't have wanted me either," I said, shaking myself loose from her hold. "I cramp his style, too."

She enfolded me in a hug I couldn't break free from. "Oh, honey," she whispered, "I didn't mean it like that. I was only joking. I'm not keeping you because it's my duty. If I had to choose between you and any man in my life, you'd always come first, you know that."

"I don't know, that's just the problem," I said, and I felt my voice cracking. "I don't seem to be first in anyone's life anymore. You don't need me and Dad doesn't need me and Grant's gone and now Pam has someone. I don't have anybody." And I started to cry, silently, on her shoulder.

She held me very close, patting me like she used to when I was a little girl and I woke from a bad dream. "I promise you, darling, that I won't rush into any relationship without thinking of you first," she said. "Any man who doesn't like my daughter can't have me. I'll get a button made and wear it all the time, how about that?"

I could feel myself laughing through my tears. "Okay," I said, "and next time I'll try to let you make up your own mind without trying to spoil things for you. And if you want to date some jerk, I'll even try to understand that."

She held me away so that she could look at my face. "I don't think you need to worry about me and some jerk," she said. "In fact, if you really want to know the truth, I hate fettuccini! It took all my willpower to eat the terrible stuff."

We looked at each other and began to laugh. Then we hugged each other hard.

Chapter 12 _____

*E*ven though my mother had reassured me that she didn't really want to keep seeing Ralph Robertson, I couldn't shake off the guilt. Every time I remembered the way I'd sat between them on the sofa and tried to turn on the TV, just like some obnoxious ten-year-old, I felt hot and cold all over. It really was as if I'd been possessed, like a character in one of Howard's movies. Soon I'd be hurling refrigerators all over the place and spinning my head around! I'd always thought I was pretty mature for my age until then. But if I hadn't thought Ralph was right for my mother, surely the mature thing to do would have been to talk it over with her, or better yet, to have waited until she discovered his faults for herself.

But maybe you don't see someone's faults when you're in love, I argued with myself. *Maybe she was really falling in love with him, and I blew it for her.* I remembered the way Joe looked at Wendy and didn't seem to notice how she was acting. I even remembered the way I had shut out all of Grant's annoying habits when I started going out with him. He had seemed perfect to me for ages—until I met Joe, in fact.

I played through a few scenes in my head: my mother sitting in her rocking chair as a lonely old woman, knitting sweaters nonstop, coming to live with me because she had nowhere else to go, and even throwing her cereal at the walls, just like Pam's grandmother. "If only she'd remarried and been happy, this never would have happened," doctors would tell me. Fifty years of guilt ahead! How would I stand it? I made up my mind to say something to Ralph the next time I saw him. I had no idea what I'd say that wouldn't sound totally dumb, but if my mother's future happiness was involved, then I didn't even mind sounding dumb for once!

But I didn't see Ralph again. Mom hardly spoke about work anymore, and I didn't think it would be wise for me to show up at the *Clarion*. If she wanted the chance to get back together with him, then I'd better stay well away.

Actually I didn't see anybody much. Now that I only worked evening shifts, I had all my days free. All those hours and nobody to share them with. I'd had no idea that days could be so long before. I rattled around the empty condo, getting hooked on soap operas and being disgusted at myself for getting hooked on them. I drove down to the beach and sunbathed a couple of times. I went to the library, and I even swam in the condo pool when it wasn't too crowded. I also scanned the want ads to see what other jobs might be available. If I wasn't having fun with my friends, I might as well be making extra money for college!

I hadn't talked to Pam all week, not since our argument on Sunday. Not having my best friend to talk to was the scariest thing of all. In my head I replayed all the good times we'd spent together: when we had flicked dough at each other when we made chocolate chip cookies and had to wash it off the walls in a hurry before my mother came home, the way we always found a spot out of the wind to eat lunch together at school, when she had offered me a huge box of Kleenex when I had finally broken down and cried after my dad moved out. She'd always been there when I'd needed her before. I wanted to be there for her now, only it seemed that she didn't need my help. Now that she had Spike, she didn't even need me at all!

My other friends from school all still lived near the country club, and although they invited me up to swim or play tennis from time to time, I hated feeling like an outsider up there, being signed into the club as someone else's guest and catching people's sorry, sympathetic looks.

Evenings were no longer a barrel of laughs either! Wendy's shift was supposed to end at five, but she had taken to hanging around and generally annoying me, too. Since she was not officially on duty, she would perch herself on the counter or one of the tables and act like Queen of the Café.

"Debbie, you are going to clean off that table in the corner, aren't you?" she'd say, in between filing her nails. "I just mentioned it in case you'd forgotten about it. It makes the place look so sloppy."

Sometimes she'd hang out in the kitchen and make similar dumb comments like, "Debbie, isn't that hamburger bun about to burn?"

There were times when I would cheerfully have tossed her onto the grill in place of a burger, but my stubborn pride, which had kept me going when I'd first started at the Heartbreak, kept me from doing anything too dumb. It was no use telling Joe how I felt. He was crazy about her, for one thing, and for another, she was very careful not to go too far with her little digs when he was around. Once, when I stomped into the kitchen and he asked me what was wrong, I exploded that I was fed up with Wendy trying to boss me around and constantly finding fault with me.

"She's only trying to help, Deb," he said. "It's just part of her nature to point out something that needs doing!"

"While she sits filing her nails and acting like she runs the place?" I demanded.

He grinned. "She's not even supposed to be on duty," he said. "She's not getting paid for being here, you know."

"Then tell her to go home!" I snapped.

He came over to me, making me take a defensive step backward. I didn't want to be influenced by his closeness anymore. "You might try to get along better with her," he said quietly. "Wendy's trying very hard to get along with you, and you're just shutting her out. It's not good for our image if we have our waitresses fighting in front of the customers, you know."

"Are you saying I should quit?" I asked.

"Of course not," he said quickly. "I'm just saying you should try a bit harder. Learn to get along with Wendy better. She's really a very nice person if you'd only give her a chance."

After that, I didn't even talk to Joe about Wendy anymore. Not that I ever saw him these days. Our conversations were limited to, "More fries and hold the pickle on that burger." If ever there was a hint of a normal conversation between us, Wendy appeared like magic, driving us both to silence. I began to look through the want ads more carefully, seeing who wanted full-time help. I hated to leave the Heartbreak after all I had gone through to fit in and learn my job, but things couldn't go on much longer the way they were. Either Wendy had to go, or I did, and with Joe on Wendy's side, it looked like I was the job hunter!

Then one evening I came to work to find Joe nowhere around and Wendy still in her apron and cap.

"Joe had to drive his grandfather home," she said. "He came in to help and then didn't feel well."

"Poor Mr. Garbarini," I said. "I wish he'd just take the summer off. It's not good for him to try to do too much in this heat."

"I told Joe not to worry, I'd cover for him," Wendy said smoothly. "I think I've got the hang of running this place by now." The way she stressed the word *running* made her meaning very clear. She was the supervisor, and I was the hired help.

"In fact," she went on, giving me one of her little smiles that didn't seem to reach her eyes, "I told Joe that if he wants to schedule some art classes this summer so he'll be ready for college in the fall, I'll take over for him."

"I see," I said. I turned my back on her and began to take my uniform from the closet.

"If you could hurry up with that, I'd appreciate it," Wendy said, still in a sugary voice. "There are tons of tables out there waiting to be cleared. We just can't have customers sitting with dirty dishes in front of them."

"Why didn't you clear them off?" I asked, trying to sound as sweet as she was.

She looked horrified. "I couldn't leave this grill, for one thing. You can't leave hamburgers in the middle of cooking them or they turn out all dry and disgusting."

I finished dressing and pinned my cap in place, then I grabbed a tray and went out to the café. Wendy wasn't kidding when she said that tables needed to be cleared off. I doubt that she'd cleared a table all afternoon. Glasses and plates were piled around the edges of tables or pyramided up in the middle while customers tried to eat between them.

"I'm sorry about this," I said at the first table, swiftly piling dishes onto the tray. "We were a person short."

I rushed from table to table, clearing away the clutter as fast as I could. Finally I staggered back to the kitchen with the Leaning Tower of Pisa on my tray. I was almost at the kitchen door when Wendy came through it.

"Watch out!" she yelled. I tried to swerve and the stack of dishes leaned too far. I watched as everything happened in slow motion. Glasses, half-drunk shakes, leftover fries, and plates cascaded toward the floor, then hit with a horrible crash. And above it all was Wendy's voice shrieking. "Now look what you've done. You've broken all that china!"

"*Me?*" I asked, already on my hands and knees picking up pieces.

"You should have known better than to try and put all that on one tray," she said, loudly enough for the whole café to hear. "You can't even do a simple job right. Joe will be so mad when he finds out. I told him he was crazy to hire you."

Slowly, like a boxer getting up from a knock-down, I staggered to my feet. "How dare you say that," I said, quietly and deliberately. "Don't you ever put me down in front of the customers again. I've had about all I can take of you. If you want that mess on the floor cleaned up, you clean it up yourself." Then I pushed past her into the kitchen.

Seconds later she followed me in. "There's going to be big trouble about this," she said. "When Joe hears that you wouldn't clean up that mess—"

"He'll wonder why you didn't do your job before I got here," I said coldly. "What were you doing all afternoon, your fingernails?"

She looked for a second as if she were going to hit me, then her expression softened again. "Look, why don't you just quit," she said. "You'll never be any good here. You're just not cut out for this sort of work. You don't belong here, acting like Miss Superior."

"I thought you told me that I was the one who belonged and you didn't," I reminded her. "I guess memory's not your strong point."

"That was before I'd been here long enough to know," she said.

"I'd say you were the one who acted like Miss Superior," I said. "I never sit around filing my nails and giving other people orders. I'd never have promoted myself to supervisor after only the first week either."

"Maybe that's because I've gotten the feel of the place quicker than you," Wendy said. "These are my sort of people, after all."

"Howard and Ashley?" I quipped. "You called them weirdos!"

A spasm of anger crossed her face. "You're deliberately being dumb," she said. "You know very well what I mean! You with your big words and your country-club manners. You're nice enough to people here, but you think you're above them. I don't know why you don't go serve croissants down at the beach."

"You'd like that, wouldn't you?" I asked. I felt deadly calm and cold, as if I were an ice sculpture. "But you won't get rid of me so easily. I was here first, and Mr. Garbarini likes me. He's still the boss, remember. He knows I'm a good worker. It's you who should go. You haven't done a decent day's work since you got here!"

"You would love for me to leave," she said, smiling—her tiger-at-lunchtime smile again. "Then you could get your little hands on Joe!"

"What?" I shouted. "What are you talking about?"

She went on smiling. "Oh, don't think I haven't noticed. I'm not blind or stupid, you know. I've seen you making little flirty eyes at him every time you think I'm out of the room. I've seen you hanging around, hoping he'll notice you. But let me tell you right now, you're wasting your time. Joe will never notice you, ever. In fact, he thinks you're really funny!"

"He does not!" I snapped.

"Oh, no?" she asked. "You should see the imitations of you he does when we're alone. 'And this is Debbie dropping hamburgers on the floor again! And here she's walking toward her car in a huff!' He thinks that all you're good for is a laugh. If you weren't so funny, he wouldn't have kept you around this long. You sure aren't worth your money as a waitress!"

I could feel the blood rush to my cheeks. I kept trying to tell myself that she was bluffing. Joe would never make fun of me behind my back. Joe did like me, even though we fought a lot!

"I don't believe you," I said. "Joe would never tell you stories just to laugh at me. You're just making it up to get me to quit."

"You don't believe it?" she asked, very sincerely now. "Then would you like an imitation of Debbie getting drunk and Joe having to drive her home and what went on afterward?"

"You're lying!" I shouted.

The smile spread across her face. "That was the funniest of all," she said. "Maybe I should go tell all the kids outside? I bet they'd all like a laugh, too!"

Suddenly something snapped. The volcano that had been building inside my head exploded. If Joe had told Wendy about that night, if he had laughed with her about it, then nothing else mattered anymore. Outraged, I grabbed the nearest thing from the counter. It was a big, ripe tomato, waiting to be sliced. I threw it at her. It hit her square in the face. It burst open, scattering tomato pulp and seeds. Wendy staggered backward, her mouth open in horror but no sound coming out, slipped on a patch of tomato seeds, and plopped down heavily on the floor.

For a moment I stared at her, horrified and delighted at the same time that I had dared to do such a terrible thing. Wendy continued to sit there while tomato juice ran down her face and the front of her shirt. She seemed too dazed and shocked to speak. Then she snapped back to reality.

"Now you've done it," she screamed. "Now you've really done it! You'd better get out of here fast, because if you don't, you're in big trouble! You just wait until Joe hears about this!"

"Actually I've already heard all I want to," Joe said as he stepped in from the back porch through the open kitchen door.

"Oh, Joe, thank goodness you're here," Wendy said, scrambling to her feet. She pointed at me. "She's a monster, Joe, she tried to kill me. Now do you see what I told you! Get her out of here!"

"Don't worry," I said, with every ounce of dignity I could muster. "I wouldn't want to stay in a place where people make fun of me behind my back. I'll go where I'm appreciated, thank you."

And with my head held very high, I stalked out of the back door. Then I kept on walking, even though my car was parked right there in the parking lot, striding out like an explorer into unknown territory. I walked right across the muddy area behind the fishermen's shacks, across the fashionable beach road with its little boutiques and upscale cafés. I still kept on walking when the houses petered out and the road began to wind up the headland to the south of Rockley Beach. I don't know where I thought I was going or what I hoped to find when I got there. But as long as I kept going, I could blot out all the pain I was feeling.

I was dimly aware of footsteps behind me, but I didn't even look back. Then I heard a voice yelling, "Debbie, wait up! Debbie, for pete's sake, slow down!" But I kept right on walking, even though the road had begun to climb steeply now.

The thudding footsteps drew closer, and Joe came alongside me, gasping for breath as he ran. "Debbie, will you please slow down?" he gasped.

I kept on walking, pretending he wasn't there.

"Debbie? Where are you going, anyway?" he demanded.

"I'm going to get a new job," I said, staring straight ahead of me and striding out with renewed strength. "One where people don't let me down."

"There's only a lighthouse at the end of this road," he said.

"So? Maybe they need an assistant lighthouse keeper," I said, still not looking at him. "Or someone to make the coffee."

"There are three hundred stairs!" he shouted as he tried to keep up with me.

"I'm not fussy. I wouldn't even mind the stairs," I said. "I hear that lighthouse keepers are very trustworthy."

Finally he grabbed my arm. "Look, Debbie, stop a minute. I have to talk to you, and I don't have any breath left," he panted. "I really don't want to die without explaining. . . ."

He held me firmly, preventing me from walking on, while he bent over, gasping and panting. "I ran all the way," he said. "Remind me never to try a marathon."

"Will you please let me go?" I asked, fighting to stay calm. "There's nothing you can say that will explain anything. Go back to Wendy and live happily ever after."

"Wendy's gone," he said.

"I don't care," I said, trying to wrench myself free of him. "Now will you—" I stopped as his words gradually sank in. "Gone where?"

He shrugged. "I don't know. Last seen walking in the direction of her car."

"So who's running the café?"

"Nobody. For all I know it's being looted and vandalized right now, and everyone in town is helping themselves to our soda."

"You've got to go back."

"Not unless you come back with me."

"You'll do fine without me," I said. "Wendy will

manage everything very well if you can find the tables under all the dishes she hasn't bussed."

He gripped my arm extra hard, swinging me toward him until I was facing him. "Don't you understand?" he shouted. "Wendy's gone."

"For good?"

He shrugged. "I don't know how good it will be yet," he said, and gave the slightest smile.

"She's really left?"

"That's right." He looked away from me, kicking a small pebble so that it bounced away down the hill. "She said that if I took your side against her, there was no point in sticking around."

"You took my side?" I asked incredulously.

"Of course I did," he said, almost shaking me. "I heard the whole thing. I had no idea she treated you like that. I would have thrown something at her a long time ago." He relaxed his hold on me. "I'm real sorry, Debbie," he said. "I should never have brought her into the café. I knew what kind of person she was. Say you'll forgive me and come back."

"So you can laugh at me behind my back again?" I demanded, suddenly furious again. "So you can do impressions of me and tell all your friends about something I thought was a secret?" I tried to fight clear of him. "Will you let go of me?" I yelled. "I don't care how bad Wendy was, it's you I can't forgive. I really thought . . . I mean, I really, really thought . . ." A sob choked to my throat. "Please let me go!" I begged.

"Not until you listen to my side!" he said, holding me more firmly. "Will you quit struggling?"

"Not until you let go of me!" I shouted.

"Ow!" he yelled as I turned and bit his arm. "Will you just stand still for one minute?"

"Are you going to let go or do I have to scream for help?" I shouted.

"I'm going to make you listen!"

"In that case I'm going to scream! *Hel*—" The word was never finished because he yanked me toward him and started kissing me hard on the mouth. I wriggled, I struggled, but part of me didn't want to struggle. I felt myself relaxing into his arms and hated myself for it.

"Was that the only way you could think of to shut me up?" I demanded as soon as he let me go.

A big grin crossed his face. "No, but it was the most fun way!" he said.

"Very funny," I snapped. "Another little detail to tell your friends about! Go ahead, have a laugh on me. I bet I even kiss funny."

"I'd say you kiss pretty well," he said. "In fact, I'd say *we* kiss pretty well." For the first time we looked at each other, his dark eyes holding my gray ones. "Debbie," he said quietly. "I never told Wendy anything about that night. I swear it. She called my house and I wasn't there. She wanted to know where I was, so I said that you'd drunk too much and I had to drive you home. That's all I said, I promise you. The rest was her imagination. She always was too jealous."

There was a long pause. The only sound was the dull thump of waves far below and the sight of the wind through the dry grass.

"She said you imitated me," I said weakly. "You made fun of me dropping hamburgers."

"I did, when you first started working," he said. "I made fun of you to your face, too, didn't I? I'm a straight kind of guy. I don't do anything behind anyone's back. If I think they're funny, I let them know, and if I like then, then I let them know that, too." He slipped his hands into mine. "I really like you, Debbie, and I think you really like me, too?"

I nodded, feeling tears well up in my eyes, so that the blue sky and yellow grass melted together into a rainbow haze behind Joe's shoulder.

"Will you come back to the café now?" he asked. "My grandfather's going to kill me if anyone walks off with the cash register!"

I stood there, staring out at the ocean, feeling the wind in my face, wrestling with the strong emotions going on inside me.

"I really need you, Debbie," Joe said quietly. "Say you'll come back."

"Okay, I guess," I said hesitantly.

A big smile broke out across his face. "That's great," he said, "because someone's got to clean all that tomato off the floor!"

He dodged nimbly aside as I lunged at him and laughed all the way back into town as I ran behind him, yelling insults he didn't seem to hear.

Chapter 13 _____

Soon things were back to normal at the Heart-break, and it was great. I got out of bed each morning looking forward to the day. It's funny how your mood can color everything, but it seemed as if summer had finally blossomed forth: every bush in every garden had suddenly sprouted flowers, the air was full of sweet scents and warm breezes, the clouds had vanished from a perfect arc of blue sky, and every fruit bowl was full of succulent peaches and plums. I sang in the shower and hummed as I made breakfast. I was happy, and I wanted everyone else to be happy, too. I wished Pam every happiness with Spike. I even wished I had not been so horrible to my mother and driven away Ralph Robertson. Maybe he had been right for her after all. Maybe in my own childishness I had refused to consider another man in her life and I had now robbed her of her one chance for happiness. I toyed with the idea of writing him a letter and explaining everything, then I decided that if fate wanted them together, it would throw them together. After all, look what it had done for Joe and me! We had started off as the world's biggest enemies, we had gradually stopped hating each other, we had come through Wendy trying to separate us forever, and now—who knew what could happen next?

Back at the café that evening we skirted around each other, treading as carefully as if the café floor were covered in eggshells. Joe had insisted on cleaning up and had treated me like a princess all evening. From time to time we would pass in the kitchen doorway and smile at each other, but we hardly said a word. It was as if neither of us was sure where the next step would lead, and neither of us was totally sure we wanted to take that next step. Once, when Joe put a hamburger patty onto a plate I was holding out for him, he said, "Debbie?"

But when I replied, "What?" he turned back to the grill again.

"Nothing. Forget it," he said.

That was near as we got to a great, meaningful conversation all evening. I don't know if he was going through the same confusion, but my head was buzzing with a million questions: Had he thrown Wendy out of the café or out of his life? Did he want me back at the café as a good, steady worker or because he liked me as a person and/or potential girlfriend? And more to the point, did I even want to take Wendy's place if it was now being offered?

I was still just as confused as I had been the first

time Joe kissed me, still not able to make up my mind about how I felt about him. One thing was certain—when he took me in his arms, something magical happened. I floated, I tingled in a way I never had with Grant. At those moments, though there had only been a few of them, and they always happened when my world was upside down, I was convinced that Joe and I were completely right for each other.

But in the cold light of day afterward, I could still see why dating Joe Garbarini might be only slightly better than going to the dentist! He was still a chauvinist, and I didn't think he could ever change. Would I ever want to go out with a boy who thought that God only created women because he had some free time on the last day of creation? Also, Joe was proud of his bluntness. Wouldn't my ideal boyfriend make me feel special and treat me as if I were perfect? Could I stay in love with a guy who roared out, "Hey, Debbie, are you trying out for a barber's pole?" when I came in wearing a striped minidress? Besides, I enjoyed our fights! Could we date and still fight at the same time?

All this was pure speculation. He was treating me very nicely, as if I'd been through a big shock, which I had, but he didn't come close to saying something like, "Hey, Deb, how about you and me going together now that Wendy's gone?"

I decided to use my own wisdom on myself. If fate wanted me to go out with Joe Garbarini, fate would arrange things somehow. In the meantime, it was kind of fun to have a new, considerate, attentive Joe around.

"It's such a nice day out there," he said one lunchtime later in the week. "You want to take a little stroll on the beach? I can handle things in here. You deserve a break today, as the competition says!" Then he laughed at his own joke.

I wasn't dumb enough to turn down the chance to walk down the beach. I'd always enjoyed feeling the warm sand under my toes, the crisp coldness of the waves that splashed over my feet. I liked the people-watching, too: little kids awestruck by their first wave or their first crab, old ladies holding up their skirts in the surf, and lovers strolling down the firm sand as if the whole beach belonged to them.

I came back refreshed and renewed, having played through a lot of dumb daydream scenes about me and Joe. Would we ever be a couple like the one in front of me, pausing to gaze at each other in wonder as we walked? I visualized myself arriving at school on the back of his motorcycle next fall, or dropping in on Grant and his friends at the lake. I also imagined his arms around me, him kissing me under the stars, and me wanting it to go on forever.

"Your friend was in here looking for you," Ashley said when I came back.

"My friend?"

"You know, kind of big. Wears a leather jacket?" Ashley said, waving her arms vaguely as she spoke.

Did Grant ever wear leather jackets? I wondered. I couldn't think of any other friends of mine who might wear leather jackets and visit me at the Heartbreak. Then Ashley added, "She said she'd be back in a minute. She went over to Terry's auto shop for a minute."

"Oh, Pam," I said. "Was she alone?"

Ashley nodded. "Pam? I thought she looked familiar. She came in here a few times, right?" She paused thoughtfully. "I remember now. She's changed a lot. I'd hardly recognize her."

I could see Ashley's point the moment Pam walked in. I, too, might have passed her in the street. Gone were the loose dresses she used to wear. Instead she had on a big leather jacket that had to be Spike's. It was old and torn in a couple of places, and it had studs around the cuffs and a giant eagle painted on the back. She was wearing tight black jeans and big boots. Her hair was slicked back. She looked almost menacing. If I'd seen her on the street at night, I'd probably have crossed to the other side.

"Hi, Deb," she said, sinking to the nearest chair. "Long time no see. How you been doing?"

"Fine," I said, cautiously. "And you?"

"Great," she said. "Will you bring me a diet soda?"

"A diet soda?" I asked. "What happened to chocolate shakes?"

She looked down modestly. "I'm trying to lose weight," she said. "Spike likes me in jeans, and jeans don't look good if you're fat. I've already lost ten pounds."

"I think you look great," I said, noticing that she really did look thinner. "I hardly recognized you."

When I came back with the soda, she was staring out of the window. "Spike's over at Terry's" she said. "We had a minor argument with a tree."

"You what?" I asked.

She grinned. "We were racing these dudes to Whitney, down the coast road, and we sort of went around a bend too fast."

"Pam!" I exclaimed in horror.

She shrugged easily. "It was fun," she said, "and we only dinged the front fender. Spike and his buddies are always doing stuff like that. We drag-raced down Fourth Street Saturday night and the cops came and we took off and they didn't catch us!"

"Pam!" I said, even more shocked. I couldn't think of anything else to say.

"What?" she asked defensively. "It's fun, Debbie," she said forcefully. "It's only fun."

"Risking your life is fun?" I asked.

"Sure, why not?" she countered. "What else is life for?"

"Plenty," I said. "And it wouldn't be much fun if you got arrested or got in a crash and wound up in a wheelchair."

She shrugged again. "That's a chance I'll take," she said. "There's nothing else happening to me that's good, that's for sure!" She paused and took a sip of her diet soda. The eyes that met mine over the rim of the glass were still sad, even though she sounded bubbly. "It's just horrible at home and nobody cares anyway," she went on, tossing back her head as though she didn't care too much either. "My grandmother's even worse, and she doesn't remember who I am any of the time now."

I nodded, trying to understand what it must be like.

"It's funny, really," she went on. "In fact, everything at home's a laugh now. My parents don't even notice I'm alive except when they want me to wipe spaghetti off the walls. Why not have fun and take risks? At least it's better than staying home. Spike is the greatest, too. He doesn't care about a thing, and he doesn't let anybody push him around. He's not even afraid of the cops or anyone."

I was staring at her hard, not quite able to believe what I was hearing. Was this the Pam I had known for ten years? The same girl who worried when we hiked on a trail marked "No Trespassing"? Who called me up a million times to find out what I was wearing to a party so that she didn't wear the wrong thing? Who never stayed out after her curfew even if the party was extra fun or the movie ran ten minutes long? Even her vocabulary had changed. It was as if she'd turned into a cardboard dummy, and someone else was speaking through her mouth.

She frowned as she picked up on my thoughts. "What's the matter?" she asked. "Are you mad at me?"

"Of course I'm not mad," I said. "You're my best friend. It's just that I get the feeling I don't know you anymore. I don't want to see you get in trouble just because you're angry at the world right now."

"I won't," she said. "Spike will take good care of

me." She smiled wide, completely transforming her face.

"So you and Spike are still going strong?" I asked. Stupid question. She smiled again.

"He's terrific, Deb."

"What do your folks think about him?"

"They don't know about him," she said. "I didn't want the hassle, so I said I was helping you out at the café."

"Thanks a lot. You might have warned me," I said.

"It's okay. They'd never check. They don't even notice I've been dressing differently. I could come down the stairs in a gorilla suit and they wouldn't even notice. It doesn't seem to matter anymore if I lie to them. They don't even listen anymore." Pam paused then, hesitating. "Uh, Debbie, can I ask you something?" She lowered her voice, looking around to see if anyone could hear.

"What?" I asked.

"About you and Grant," she said. "Did you ever, you know, go all the way?"

"No, of course not!" I said hastily. "With Grant? Are you crazy? He almost had to ask permission to hold my hand."

"Oh," she said, looking disappointed. "I just wondered, that's all."

She played with her straw, looking down at the table. I felt I had to say something. "Has Spike asked you to?"

She twirled the straw around furiously. "Sort of," she said. "His friends all do it with their girlfriends. He knows I'm kind of backward, so he hasn't rushed me, but last night he told me that I would if I loved him."

"That's the oldest line in the book," I said. "Besides, how can you tell if you love the guy after just a couple of weeks?"

"I guess you could tell right away if you'd found the right guy for you," she said. "I just don't know, Debbie. I'm all confused. Maybe I do love him, maybe he is the right guy for me. Maybe I am being unfair by stalling. I'm so new at all this. He says that everyone does it these days. Maybe I'm being old-fashioned."

"Because you don't want to, you mean?" I asked.

"I don't know whether I want to or not," she said, louder than she intended, then looked embarrassed. "I just don't know," she repeated. "But I do know one thing—I'm not going to risk losing Spike."

"So you're going to let yourself be pressured into something you're not sure of, just to keep a guy you're not sure you even like?" I demanded. "That's pretty dumb if you ask me."

"We might all be dead tomorrow," she said, suddenly aggressive again. "Who knows what will happen? Look at my grandmother. She had this great house, she used to play bridge and tennis and volunteer. She was always busy, and now look at her. She's not even a person anymore. She's a vegetable, something you have to feed every four hours and bathe once a day. I think Spike is right—you have to get your fun while you can."

I coughed uneasily. "You're talking about more than fun, Pam. You're talking about major involvement. Promise me you'll think this over carefully. You don't want to find yourself stuck with a small-town dropout, no matter how nice you think he is right now."

Pam got to her feet. "Maybe I like being stuck with him," she said. "Here's the money for the soda. Terry's here. Be talking to you, Debbie."

Then she walked out, leaving me feeling that I handled the whole scene the completely wrong way. She must have been asking for help or she'd never have brought the subject up. Now I'd just driven her away. But I honestly didn't know how to reach her now without sounding like I was preaching. Everything I tried to say to her wound up sounding like a lecture. I didn't mean it to, but I just didn't know how to handle any of this Spike business. I did know one thing, though—unless somebody did something real soon, Pam was going to wind up in big trouble.

The trouble was that I was no smarter on the subject of guys than she was. Grant and I had not gone further than good-night kisses, which had been enough for me and, apparently, enough for him. I'd liked those kisses, but I didn't know how I would have reacted if he'd wanted more. Would I have agreed to something I wasn't sure of, just to make sure I didn't lose him? I didn't think so, but then, I'd never been totally in love with Grant. I'd been proud and happy to have him as my boy-friend, but he'd been more of a status symbol than a friend. So I'd never been in the position Pam was in now. If I were ever faced with a guy who made my legs turn to jelly, then maybe I'd know how she felt.

Joe came out of the kitchen right then, looked around, and saw me at the table. "Are you on strike, or what?" he said. "Get back in here. It's a lonely life cooking hamburgers all by myself." Then he smiled at me.

Joe, for example, I said to myself as I got up. I knew that when Joe had kissed me, I'd wanted it to go on forever. I'd even asked him to stay when he brought me home. What if he had?

"You guys are all alike," I said as I picked up a towel and began drying things in the kitchen. "You only think about one thing."

"Hamburgers?" he asked, looking wary and confused.

"You know very well it's not hamburgers!" I snapped.

He looked even more confused. "Debbie? Did I say something I didn't know I said?" he asked.

"Not yet, but you might," I answered, "and then I wouldn't know what to say back."

He looked at me, then shook his head. "I think I'd better go get Wendy back," he said. "At least I knew what she was talking about. Herself, most of the time, but at least I could understand her."

He looked genuinely confused standing there, almost helpless for once, and very appealing. I grinned. "I'm sorry," I said. "I was mad at all boys. You haven't done anything. Just don't get Wendy back."

Chapter 14 ─────────

That night I found that my insides still felt tied in knots every time I thought about Pam. I kept remembering that big leather jacket, the slicked-back hair, and the things she kept saying about not caring and having fun. Did she really mean them, or was she just trying to convince herself? I curled into a ball, feeling cold and scared, and just wished there was someone I could talk to about her. It was no good telling my mom—who'd only say that I should phone Pam's folks right away—because that would make Pam hate me forever. I'd started to tell Joe, but I got all embarrassed in the middle. Anyway, I knew exactly what he'd say. He'd say that I should butt out and let Pam do her own thing.

If only her parents knew what she was going through, maybe they'd do something to help, I thought. If only I could let them know what she was feeling, without letting on too many details about Spike, then they could let her know that they hadn't forgotten her. I wished I dared call them.

138

As it turned out, I never had to make that phone call. That night I dreamed that Pam was standing on the edge of a cliff, far too near the edge, and it was up to me to rescue her. The trouble was that I was scared of falling myself. I inched my way toward that terrible drop, and as I did so the edge of the cliff began to crumble. Great chunks of land fell away, bouncing down the cliff with a thumping sound, thumps that got louder and louder until . . . I opened my eyes and tried to wake up in a hurry. The rattling of pebbles was still going on in the darkness. Then it came to me: someone was knocking on my window.

Very cautiously I slid out of bed and peeked through the blinds. The trouble with a ground-floor condo unit was that almost anyone could be outside. Maybe someone had our unit mixed up with someone else's. Maybe the lady next door had gone out for a secret two A.M. rendezvous. I half expected to see a drunk or some kids playing pranks out there. Instead, Pam's scared face was peering in, only a few inches from my own. I jumped a mile at the closeness of the face, then, when I had recovered, I slid open the window.

"You scared me half to death," I said. "Honestly, I thought my heart was going to stop."

"Sorry. I had to talk to you. I thought you'd never wake up and someone else would hear me," she whispered.

"We have a perfectly good doorbell," I said.

"I know, but I didn't want to wake your mother up," she said.

"Is something wrong?"

"Something terrible's happened. I couldn't go home. I had to talk with someone. Can I come in?"

"Of course you can," I said. I pulled back the blinds and helped her slither in. Once she was inside, she collapsed onto my bed, shivering violently.

"Here," I said, wrapping my robe around her shoulders. "It's okay. You're all right now."

She went on shaking. "I'm sorry I woke you up," she managed to say at last. "I couldn't think of what else to do."

"So what happened?"

"I don't know what to do," she said again.

"Was it Spike?" I asked. "Did he try to force you. . . ."

She shook her head. "No. It was nothing to do with me, except I was in the car with him. He hit somebody, Debbie."

"He what?" I yelled. I had tried to be calm, but I hadn't been expecting anything like this.

"Keep your voice down," Pam whispered. "We can't let your mother hear."

"What happened, exactly?" I asked, trying not to envision armed gang members bursting through my front door, silencing Pam and me in a hail of machine-gun fire because we knew too much.

She let out a great, shuddering sigh. "We were driving home along Hidden Valley Road. Spike was driving fast, the way he always does, and then, suddenly, we came around this corner in the middle of the road. A car was coming in the other direction. It tried to swerve out of our way, but there was no room. Then there was this terrible crunch, and the other car went off the road. Spike sort of slowed down like he was going to stop, then he looked back and sped up again. I grabbed his arm and yelled, 'Aren't you going to help them?' And Spike said something like, 'Are you crazy? Let's get out of here fast, before anyone sees us.'

"We drove real fast. Spike was really scared. He kept saying, 'Hey, they can't pin this on me. There's no evidence. They'll never know.' I kept thinking of those people in that car. What if they were hurt? I said we should call the police when we got to Rockley Beach, and he got angry. I was so scared, Debbie. I came right over here." She buried her head into her hands and began to cry. "What if someone's hurt bad, Debbie? What am I going to do?"

"Um, let's just stay calm, okay? First, we've got to make sure those people from the other car are okay. Do you want to drive back to where it happened?" I asked.

She nodded. "We could do that," she said. "They wouldn't question us or anything, would they? We'd just be passersby."

"I think so," I said. "Just wait a minute while I put on some jeans."

I got dressed in a hurry and scribbled a note to my mother in case she woke up and found me gone. "Driving Pam home. She had car trouble," it said, which was sort of true.

I was shaking so hard that I could hardly hold the steering wheel as we drove slowly down Hidden Valley Road. The road was not very well lit. I could barely see, and I kept trying to picture what

I would do if we found the car and the people in it were badly hurt. I tried to remember the first aid we had taken in school, and the only thing that came back was how to treat sunburn. Was I really strong enough and brave enough to face this? Pam sat beside me, perched nervously on the edge of her seat, staring out the front window.

"I think it was near here," Pam said hesitantly. "I remember there was a big oak tree on the bend."

We came around the curve and slowed to a crawl. Sure enough, the headlights picked up a streak of skid marks, but at the end of them there was nothing. We stopped the car and got out. Still nothing.

"Maybe they were okay," I said. "Maybe they were only shaken up and they drove off again."

"Maybe," she said. "But there was this terrible crunch. We must have hit them real bad."

"Maybe the police and ambulance have already been here," I said, "and anyone who got hurt is safely in the hospital by now."

"I guess so," she said, still pacing up and down and searching through the bushes. "I have to find out for sure. Don't you see? I could have made Spike go for help. I could have made him stop. I could have gotten out and flagged down another car. I could have done more, only I didn't want to go against Spike. I didn't want to upset him, Debbie. I still cared what he thought."

"And you don't now?"

She looked away, past me into the night. "Debbie, he didn't care that he might have killed somebody. All he thought was about saving himself.

Gee, I sure had him all wrong. I thought he was strong. I thought he'd take care of me, but he was a wimp after all." She gave a choked sob. "I can't believe how stupid I was. What a dummy."

I reached out and gently touched her arm. "No, you're not."

She smiled weakly. "I guess we'd better call the police now." I nodded. "Do you think we could call them anonymously, so Spike won't know it was me? I'd feel kind of awful if he knew."

"Sure. We can even do it from the nearest phone booth. Then they can't trace the call."

"Boy, we're already starting to think and talk like criminals, aren't we?" Pam said with a very shaky laugh. "See what having me for a friend has done—I'm dragging you into a life on the run."

"Come on, you nut," I said, laughing. "I bet we're both worrying for nothing."

She nodded. A car passed, its headlights cutting a beam of light through the darkness. It didn't slow as it passed us. Pam shivered again. "Let's get out of here," she said. "This place gives me the creeps."

I shivered, too. I took her arm. "Let's just hope for the best, Pam," I said. "Let's hope that everything's going to be okay, okay?"

Pam was still shivering as she got back into the car. "What if the police say that someone was hurt badly? Should I tell them it was us?"

"I guess you're going to have to," I said. "Even though it'll be hard, you've got to tell them." We drove along silently in the darkness. I didn't know what Pam was thinking, but I was thinking about what the police would do if they found out. Would she get in trouble for being an accessory? I knew what was right—to phone the police and confess— but that didn't make it any easier.

Chapter 15 _____

My fingers were numb with cold and shaking; I could hardly dial the number of the police. I had promised Pam I would do it for her, and now I sincerely wished I hadn't. What if they asked me how I knew about the accident? What if they traced the call and they had a patrol car in the area and before we had come out of the booth they had surrounded us with searchlights?

"Police department," said a calm, efficient-sounding woman.

"I'm calling about . . . I mean, I wondered if an accident has been reported on Hidden Valley Road tonight?" I stammered. My tongue didn't want to work.

"One minute please, I'm transferring you," the calm voice said, and I had to repeat my question for the next person I talked to.

"Hidden Valley Road . . . yes, there was an accident. The report's just been filed," the impersonal voice said. "Were you a witness, young lady?"

"Me? Uh, no, I was . . . just told about it. I, er,

145

friends of mine were driving that way, and I wondered if anyone was hurt. I was worried about my friends."

"I see," the policeman said, sounding as if he didn't believe me. I could imagine the call being traced at this moment. I heard him turning pages. "Blue Nissan, license DYP-833," he said. "Was that your friends?"

"I'm, er, not sure," I said. "Was anyone hurt?"

"One woman was taken to Valley General with unknown injuries," he said. "No report of young people injured."

I hung up and stood there trembling.

"A woman was taken to Valley General with unknown injuries," I said. "And they got Spike's license-plate number. That means they know he did it. He'll probably be charged with leaving the scene of an accident," I added gently.

"I don't care about Spike now. What happened to the woman?"

"I don't know. He said her injuries were unknown."

"I have to go to Valley General, Debbie. I have to find out how she is."

"Okay," I said. "Next stop, General Hospital."

We parked in the visitor's lot at General and walked up the impressive flight of steps to the front entrance. Our feet echoed across the marble entrance hall. It was very big and imposing, and we were both terrified. In the car on the way over we had tried to work out a reason for asking questions. The plan we came up with sounded perfect in the car, but now I didn't know whether we could go through with it.

"Can I help you, young ladies?" the woman at the front desk asked. She looked friendly enough.

"We, er, we'd like to inquire about a patient," I said.

"Visiting hours are from two P.M.—"

"I know. I just need to know if she's all right."

"I'll check. Room number?"

"I, er, don't know that."

"Okay. Name?"

"I, uh, don't know that either."

"You don't know the patient's name?" she asked, looking at us suspiciously. "Why would you want to visit somebody you don't know?"

"My friend is trying to check on a lady who was in a car accident tonight. She was hurt and my friend saw the car and thought it might be this nice old lady who lives down the street and drives a car just like that and she lives all alone and there will be nobody to take care of her cats if she's in the hospital."

I knew I was babbling. I could hear my voice going on and on and on. The woman was looking at me curiously.

"Can't your friend speak for herself?" she asked, looking across at Pam.

"I get nervous," Pam said, at exactly the same time that I said, "She gets nervous."

The woman shook her head. She scanned a list in front of her. "So she was admitted tonight, right?"

"Right," we both said.

"About what age was she?"

I said seventy-five at the same time that Pam said fifty-nine.

The woman looked at us curiously again. "There was one accident victim brought in. Mrs. Betty Carlisle. Room 33B. Could that be her?"

We both half nodded.

"How old is she?" Pam blurted out. "Is she all right?"

"I just have the name and room number. I don't get hourly bulletins," the woman said impatiently. "It's almost midnight. No visitors are allowed now. You'd better come back and visit in the morning."

"Thank you," we mumbled. We pretended to walk toward the front door, then scooted around the corner toward the elevators.

"We're not supposed to be here now," I whispered to Pam. My heart was hammering so loudly I thought the sound would echo down the tiled hall. "What do we say if they stop us?"

"Whatever floor we're on, we claim we're looking for something else—say we're trying to find the lab or the women's bathroom or something," she said. "I have to know, Debbie. Don't chicken out on me now."

We pressed the elevator button and stood there in the big, empty hallway, feeling very naked and exposed as messages boomed out over the intercom system. The elevator seemed to take forever.

"What do we do if we actually come face-to-face with this woman?" I asked. "Go up and shake her hand and say, 'Hi, I'm the one who ran you off the road'?"

"We'll just make sure she's going to be okay, then we'll run for our lives," Pam said.

We came to a deserted hallway and crept down it, keeping close to the wall.

"I bet we look like a couple of spies," I said.

"I bet we look totally stupid," she answered, "but I sure don't want to have to do any more explaining."

"This is it," I whispered, pausing outside a half-open door marked 33B. "Should we go in?"

"Are you crazy? What can you see through the crack in the door?"

"Nothing but the end of a bed."

At that moment we heard brisk footsteps coming down the hall.

"Hide," Pam whispered, dragging me into a doorway on the other side of the hall.

"Why?" I shot back.

"Because."

Two orderlies in green walked down the hall beside a nurse. We cowered in the doorway. "In here," we heard her say. "Over by the window."

"Only brought in tonight?" one orderly asked.

"Yes. Wasn't even rated code blue," the nurse went on. "Quite a surprise, in fact. They want to do an autopsy. The doctor wasn't happy about the probable cause of death."

"Death?" Pam gasped in my ear. We shrank back into the shadows as the figures opened the door wide and went in. A few minutes later they came out again. This time they were pushing a trolley covered in a white sheet. They left it out-

side a service elevator and disappeared back into
the room again.

"Quick," Pam whispered, "we've got to do something quick."

"Like what?"

"Hide the body. Get it out of here. We can't let
them do the autopsy."

She began to run forward. "Are you crazy?" I
said, springing after her. Obviously she was. A sane
person would not consider hiding a long trolley
with a heavy body on it.

"Help me push it," she said. "Maybe we can lock
it in a closet or something, or file it in a filing cabinet. I won't want to wind up in San Quentin for
the rest of my life."

"You won't," I said dryly. "That's a men's jail."

I grabbed her arm. "Leave it alone. Come on.
There's nothing you can do."

"What are you doing?" A nurse's voice boomed
down the hall behind us.

She hurried up to us, frowning suspiciously.
"What were you doing with that trolley," she demanded.

"We, er . . ." I stammered. "It, uh, it was her
aunt. She wanted to take a last look at her."

"Her aunt?"

"Yes. They were very close."

The nurse continued to look suspiciously. "I
hardly think it was her aunt," she said. "You must
have made a mistake. This was a twenty-five-year-
old man. Brought in with a brain hemorrhage."

"A man? With a brain hemorrhage?" we both
blurted out together.

"We thought it was Betty Carlisle," I managed to say.

"She was in a car accident," Pam added.

"And she's your aunt?"

"Sort of. My aunt once removed, on my mother's side," Pam said. I started to giggle. I was so cold and scared and tense I couldn't help myself.

The nurse frowned. "Is this some sort of prank?" she asked.

"Oh, no," we both said in unison again.

"She just wants to know if Betty Carlisle is okay," I said. "She saw the accident."

"Sort of saw it," Pam added. "Was told about it, actually."

The nurse picked up the chart beside the door. "Kept overnight with concussion," she said. "She has a couple of cuts on her forehead, too, but she'll be fine."

"Oh, that's wonderful," Pam said, a big grin spreading across her face. "I'm so glad she's only got a concussion. I mean, I'm not glad she's got a concussion, but I'm glad it wasn't something worse."

The nurse almost smiled, too. "She's sleeping and under observation," she said. "Do you want me to tell her you called?"

"Oh, er, no thanks, that's all right," Pam said. "We'd better get home now. Thank you very much."

We grabbed each other and ran back down the hall. Once in the elevator, we looked at each other.

"Pam Paulson," I said, "I don't ever want to go

through something like that again for as long as I
live."

"Don't worry," she said. "From now on I go back
to being my old boring self. No more midnight ad-
ventures. No more fast driving—"

"And no more stealing bodies in hospitals," I
said. "Honestly, Pam, if anyone had told me this,
I'd never have believed it!"

"I still don't believe it," she said. "And all those
dumb things I did with Spike. What on earth made
me act like that, Debbie?"

"I understand why you did it," I said. "You were
scared and hurt that your family was turned upside
down over your grandmother. You were trying to
make them notice you. Little kids do the same
thing when they have tantrums to get their own
way."

She looked embarrassed. "Are you saying I'm no
better than a little kid?" she asked. "And I thought
I was so mature."

The elevator stopped and we stepped out into
the empty foyer. "You're not the only one who
acts childish under stress," I said. "I think we all
do. You should have seen me acting like a total
brat trying to get rid of my mom's new boyfriend.
I still blush when I think about it."

"Really?" she asked. "You didn't tell me about
that."

"Because I was too mortified afterward," I said.
"I couldn't even believe it was me who had acted
that way. I even slid in between them on the sofa!"

Pam started to smile. "You did? Seriously?"

I nodded. "I'll tell you all about it on the way home."

She touched my arm shyly. "You're a good friend, Debbie," she said. "I'm glad I've got you around."

"I didn't think I was good enough," I said. "I wanted to help you, but I didn't know what to do. I felt so helpless watching you going in what I thought was the wrong direction."

"You did try to warn me," she said. "I just wasn't ready to listen. I had to find out a few things for myself. I learned my lesson, though. This was the worst night of my life, but it did make me realize something."

"About Spike?" I asked.

"More than that," she said. "It made me realize that life is special. All life. When I thought about that car going off the road and people maybe getting killed, I knew then that whatever Spike said, those people mattered." She paused as I opened the heavy swinging door, then stepped through it. "It made me think again about my grandmother," she said. "It made me realize that it isn't her fault she doesn't know me anymore. I've been angry at her for changing, and it's not her fault. I'm going to try harder with her, Debbie, try to still love her even though she's hard to love right now."

We linked arms and walked together down the steps and toward my car.

Chapter 16 ─────────────

I thought Pam had been through enough that night to last a lifetime. Now that Spike was out of her life, I certainly wasn't expecting any more desperate phone calls from her. So I was completely unprepared when I picked up the phone a few mornings later.

"Debbie?" Pam said in a tense voice. "Are you busy?"

"I'm busy opening both eyes," I said. "I was sleeping in for once."

"Do you think you could come over?" she asked. "I really need you." Her voice wobbled alarmingly.

"What's going on?" I asked, half-dreading the answer. Spike's gang had threatened to get her, and she wanted me to join her in the shoot-out, or she'd just discovered she was pregnant, or . . .

"It's my grandmother," Pam said.

I let out a heavy sigh of relief. Grandmothers I could cope with.

"They're coming to take her to the home today.

154

A bed just became available. My mother has to work, and she asked me to pack all of Grandma's things. I don't want to do it alone, Debbie. Could you come over?"

"Sure," I said. "I'll be right there."

"Thanks," she said, "I really didn't want to do it alone."

"I understand," I said. "See you in about half an hour."

Pam met me at the door. "There's really not that much to do," she said. "It's just that, for some reason, I'm finding it very hard."

I gave her my biggest smile. "We'll get it done quickly and then I'll take you down for lunch at the Heartbreak," I said.

Pam turned to lead me up the stairs. "Grandma fell last night," she whispered. "The doctor came and put her under sedation."

Pam led the way into what used to be her bedroom. It was now almost fully taken up by a hospital bed, both side-rails now up and a tiny little old woman sleeping in the middle of it. Pam already had a large suitcase open on the floor and was taking items out of the dresser drawers.

"I wonder if she'll ever use these things again," she said. "I guess I'd better pack them, but ..." She held up a pair of sturdy walking shoes. "We used to walk for miles," she said, smiling at the memory. "She'd walk to the grocery store and wheel her groceries home in a wire cart. She never took the car unless she had to."

"Pack everything," I said. "You never know—

they're coming out with new miracle cures every day."

Pam shook her head. "I know that when she goes out through that door, I'll never see her again," she said quietly. "I just know it."

"You can go downstairs if you'd like," I said. "I don't mind doing this alone if it upsets you."

"It's all right," she said. "It's really my job." She took a folded apron tenderly from the bottom drawer. "She always wore this when she was baking," she said. "You should have tasted her homemade brownies," she said. "And bread, too. She liked to bake her own bread. She used to make me my own little loaf, just the right size for me."

At the sound of our voices, the old woman stirred and moaned. Pam rushed over to her. "It's all right, Grandma. It's just me."

Two bright blue eyes opened and looked at Pam, then the old woman frowned. "Oh, it's you come back again, is it?" she asked. "You never leave me alone, do you, Hettie?"

Pam looked across at me. "She still thinks I'm her sister," she said. "The one who died when she was young."

To her grandmother she said patiently, "I'm Pam, Grandma. I'm your granddaughter."

The eyes narrowed, then opened wider again. "So you are," the little, cracked voice said. "Little Pammie. How did you get to be so big? You were just a little thing."

"I grew up, Grandma," Pam said. "I'm seventeen years old now."

"Little Pammie, all grown up," the old voice said.

"Where did the years go?" She turned around and saw the half-packed case. "What are you doing with my things?"

"You hurt yourself when you fell down," Pam said gently. "They want to take you into the nursing home until you get better."

The old woman raised her head to get a better look. "I'm not going to need my walking shoes in a nursing home," she said.

Pam smiled. "Just in case," she said. "I want you to practice walking so that we can go on long walks again, like we used to."

Her grandmother nodded. Then she beckoned to Pam. "I want you to open that top drawer," she whispered. "You'll find a little box on the right-hand side."

Pam opened the drawer and brought out the cardboard box.

"Give it to me," the old woman commanded. She took the top off and brought out a pin, made in the shape of a rose. It was rather a gaudy pin made of bright colored enamel, and it had an old-fashioned look to it. But the old woman held it up tenderly, smiling as she looked at it. "I want you to keep this, Pammie," she said to her granddaughter. "Just in case I don't come back from the home. I want you to have it. You'd understand."

"Did Grandpa give it to you?" Pam asked, taking it gently as the old woman held it out to her.

A lovely, warm smile crossed her creased face. "The day he asked me to marry him," she said. "It was at the county fair. He won it for me at the shooting gallery. He sort of shoved it into my hand

and said, 'This had better last you a good long while, because I won't have any money to spare for frivolous things like flowers if I'm to build you a house.'

"And I said, 'If you want to start building me a house, hadn't you better ask me to marry you first?' And he blushed like a schoolboy."

Her face had become almost like a young girl's again. Her eyes sparkled, and her cheeks were pink as she relived that moment. "I've always kept it safe and taken it everywhere with me since then. I even rescued it first when we had a fire," she added.

"Then take it to the home with you," Pam said. "You could wear it. . . ."

The old woman shook her head. "When they go through my things, they won't know the value of it and they'll just throw it out with the garbage," she said. "You'll keep it safe for me, won't you?"

Pam nodded. "I'll keep it safe, Grandma," she whispered, and leaned over the railing to kiss the old woman. When she turned away, I could see that she was crying. I hurried to finish the packing for her. I felt all strange inside, as if I'd been privileged to witness a miracle or something. Pretty soon after that the ambulance arrived with Pam's parents. The old woman's face was bewildered again as she was carried out. Pam wouldn't go downstairs to see her off. We sat together in the empty room.

"I'm so glad she knew me," Pam said, pausing to brush the tear from her cheek. "Now I can always remember her like this and not like . . . the other times."

I nodded. I didn't know what to say.

She put her arm around my shoulder. "And I'm so glad you were here to share it with me, Debbie."

"You want to go to the Heartbreak?" I asked. "For a double chocolate madness?"

She got to her feet. "I'm not sure about the Heartbreak, Deb," she said. "Strange things happen to people when they go there. How about McDonald's instead?"

I laughed. "Okay. McDonald's if you want," I said. "Although they don't know a thing about chocolate madnesses."

Chapter 17 _____

I tried hard to be there for Pam for the first few days after her grandmother went away. I got off work early one evening and we went to a movie. I took a long lunch hour and we went to the beach. It was pretty much like old times, and it felt great to have a friend around again.

"You know, nothing's fun if you've got nobody to share it with," I said after we had both been dunked by a big wave and wound up spluttering and laughing on the shore. "I'm glad you didn't wind up as a lady Hell's Angel."

"Me, too," she said. "Tight jeans and big jackets are not the most comfortable things in the world to wear."

After the beach I persuaded her to drop in at the Heartbreak with me. Things got rather busy, and Pam offered to help out. She was terrific, calmly taking orders and cleaning off tables. Joe and I looked at each other as if the answer to our pray-

160

ers had just landed. When we suggested that she might like to work there, she seemed pleased.

"She doesn't even mind cleaning the bathroom floor," I whispered to Joe. "Slight change from Wendy!"

He looked at me rather thoughtfully. "You know, Wendy wasn't all bad," he said. "You just saw the bad side of her. Oh, I admit she thought about herself most of the time, but she did know how to make a guy feel special."

"Are you having second thoughts about breaking up with her?" I asked, and hoped that my voice didn't give too much away.

I thought he hesitated before he answered, but then he grinned and said, "Not really. She was great looking and all that, and she did like to fuss over me—you know, cook my favorite meals for me, give me back rubs. . . ." His eyes became all dreamy, then he shook his head. "But it all got to be a bit much. It felt like I was her pet dog sometimes. You know, I like to run my own life . . . *and* choose my own clothes."

I thought about that conversation as I cleaned off the tables. I guess I'd never thought of Joe missing Wendy before. I was so relieved to have her out of the way that I had forgotten she and Joe had been close to each other for quite a while. He had said she knew how to make a guy feel special. I had a feeling he was hinting that I couldn't do that. I had even laughed at the way Wendy hung around Joe and fluttered her eyelashes at him. It had never occurred to me before that he actually liked that stuff! Not that I could ever pout and bat my eyelashes; I just wasn't made that way. But it wasn't good for my ego to realize that I didn't measure up to Wendy in some things.

"What's wrong?" Pam asked. "You're gazing out into space all the time. Are you having a vision?"

"Just thinking," I said, glancing into the kitchen.

"About Joe?"

I nodded.

"Has he asked you out yet?"

"Not yet," I answered.

"But you'd go if he did, wouldn't you?"

I sighed. "I don't know, Pam. I guess I would, but I don't know if it would be such a smart idea. You know how different we are. We disagree about almost everything. He annoys me so much at times that I want to barbecue him instead of the hamburgers. And yet . . ."

"And yet you still really like him," Pam put in. "That is totally obvious. When you two are together, there is so much electricity in the air—we could save money and run the french fryer on the charge that's flashing between you."

I laughed, a little embarrassed. "But he hasn't even suggested going out together," I said. "Maybe he just likes me as a good waitress, that's all."

"I doubt it," Pam said. "Maybe he doesn't know how to change the way things are between you."

"He's certainly being cautious, isn't he?" I agreed. "We're not even fighting so much these days."

I wasn't sure if this was a good sign or a bad sign. When we were together, we skirted around each other, not like two boxers anymore, but more like two big-game hunters, pursuing unknown wild animals. I could feel the tension, and it left me on edge and confused. When I was alone, I wondered if I hadn't imagined our feelings for each other. Maybe Joe didn't care about me at all. Maybe he thought he had come on a little too strong when he stopped me from walking out on him, and now he regretted it. I just wished I knew. If he really liked me, as a girl as opposed to as a waitress, why didn't he say something? Didn't guys who liked girls ask them out to movies or to dance? Especially guys like Joe who were so sure of themselves and their own masculine charms. It would have been more in character if he'd told me it was my turn to be his girlfriend and it was a great honor. Not saying anything and being polite just wasn't like Joe. And yet, sometimes he looked at me in such a special way that I just knew he had to be feeling the same way I did.

Toward the end of Pam's first week, the two German boys showed up again. They had popped in from time to time after surfing and always chatted with me. This time they came in with Art, our resident surfing bum, and I was able to introduce them to Pam.

"Ve are getting to be ze great surfing dudes, ja?" Klaus asked Art.

"Oh, sure," Art said. He turned to me. "They've finally learned which side of the board is up!" he whispered with a grin. "And they haven't mown anybody down recently, which is a miracle."

He slapped Klaus on the back. "You've got the best teacher on the coast," he said. "No way you could fail to learn. When you go home, you can tell them Art taught you everything you know."

"You are being most kind to us," Pieter agreed.

"So how about treating your poor starving teacher to a burger?" Art asked. He was the greatest con artist when it came to not paying for food.

"Oh, sure, Art," Klaus said. "Nothing is too good for my buddy Art, who teaches me ze riding of hosepipes."

"Pipeline," Art said, furrowing his forehead in despair.

"Hey, Debbie," he called. "Bring a double cheeseburger and fries for me and my buddies. And extra-large root beer floats!"

I went into the kitchen with the order. Joe was busy chopping tomatoes.

"The German boys are in again," I said, "and Art has conned them into buying him food."

Joe nodded. "So what else's new?" he asked.

I made the floats and carried them out.

"Debbie, come sit beside me," Klaus insisted. "I am so lonely. All day I am looking forward to seeing my Debbie again."

"I have to work," I said, feeling myself blush. "Why don't you talk to Pam? She's on her break."

"Oh, you have brought ze friend. How nice," Klaus said, beaming at her. "Ze two cute American chicks. We can make ze dopple date, eh, Pieter?"

"Good idea," Pieter said, also beaming first at Pam and then at me. "Vat you like to do, go to ze bowling? Ze movies? Eating ze pizza?"

"I'd better see if your orders are ready," I said,

turning away toward the kitchen. Joe was putting fries on the plates.

"Those German boys just invited Pam and me on a double date," I said.

"That's nice," Joe said, not looking around.

"You think I should go?" I asked.

"If you want to, I guess," he said. We were skirting around each other again. He sounded completely casual, as if we were discussing the weather. "If you think it's right for you," he added.

"Why shouldn't it be right for me?" I asked. I waited for him to say, *Because you like me better. Because I don't want you to date another guy.*

"Lots of reasons," he said. "Germans like doing all this hearty outdoor stuff."

"So? I like outdoor stuff, too."

"Then it's fine, I guess," he said. "You don't have to get my permission, you know."

"I wasn't getting your permission," I said coldly. "I wasn't sure whether I wanted to go out with them, and I was just getting a second opinion."

There was a pause. "So what do you think?" I asked. "They're waiting for me to answer. I don't see why not, do you?"

I thought he hesitated. Then he said, "Er, no, I don't see why not either. If you like hiking over mountains and yodeling."

"They were thinking more of movies or pizza," I said.

"I see," he said.

"You think it would be okay to go to a movie with them?"

"If you want to," Joe said, still sounding casual.

"If you don't mind a totally boring evening. They are a bit juvenile, aren't they?"

"I think they're funny," I said. "They have a good sense of humor."

"Then go," Joe said. "You're a big girl now. You can take care of yourself. You can wrestle them away in the backseat when they come on too strong. I understand Germans are very physical."

He did look around then.

"Maybe I might not want to wrestle them off," I said.

"This order is ready," he said, putting the plate down noisily on the counter.

"Thank you," I said.

I walked back out with the orders.

"So you and Pam come to the movies with us?" Klaus asked again.

I glanced over my shoulder to see Joe's shadow, moving across the kitchen. Was it my imagination or had he moved to be able to hear better? He was no longer standing at the grill.

"I think it might be fun, don't you, Pam?" I asked.

"Oh, yes, sure, great," Pam said.

"Great," I said. "We'll come."

"All is great then," Pieter said, beaming at us. "We have ze great evening. Lots of fun together."

"That's right," I said. "Lots of fun together."

Back in the kitchen I heard Joe close a cabinet, none too gently.

I hope I'm doing the right thing, I thought, trying to take part in a light conversation while half my concentration was on what was going on in the kitchen behind me. *I hope this makes Joe realize that if he doesn't ask me, somebody else will.* Then another thought struck me. *I hope he doesn't think I really like one of the German boys better than him!*

Chapter 18 ⸻⸻⸻⸻⸻

"**W**hy does love have to be so complicated?" I asked Pam. We had gone out with the Germans. They were polite and perfect escorts all evening, and we had had a good time, even if, as Joe had predicted, it was a little boring. Joe had not asked me about the date, but he had seemed to be in a bad mood ever since.

Pam smiled. "Would you rather be like an amoeba and simply split down the middle to reproduce than go through all this stuff with boys?" she asked.

I nodded. "Sometimes that seems like a good idea," I said. "Humans have to play too many games. Why can't we come right out and say 'I like you. Do you like me?'"

"Yeah, why can't we?" Pam concurred. "There doesn't seem to be any reason why not."

"Because we don't all want to look like fools," I said. "Or, at least, in my case, because *I* don't want to look like a fool. I mean, I'm not one hundred percent sure he likes me. You know what my imagination is like. Maybe I've been reading too much into all the things he's said to me. Maybe Joe is the kind of guy who doesn't mind kissing a girl when there's an opportunity but doesn't think it means much."

"I wish you guys would settle things either way," Pam said. "All this electricity is making my hair full of static!"

"Maybe we're just imagining that, too," I said. "Maybe the only tension around here is Joe missing Wendy."

"Anyone missing Wendy would not look at a girl the way Joe looks at you," Pam said wisely. "I think you two should talk things out, and soon."

"I don't know. . . ." I said. "What if I go out with him and it's a big mistake and we ruin things forever and we're not even friends anymore and I have to find a new job and—"

Pam interrupted this orgy of self-torture with a big, exaggerated sigh. "I wish you'd make up your mind. One minute you're in despair because he's not chasing you, the next you're saying that you don't know whether you'd want him if he caught you!"

"That's right," I agreed. "Remind me to come back as an amoeba in my next life. Then I'll just split in two and shut up."

"I think the Amazons had the best idea," Pam put in. "They learned to live completely without men."

"Not totally without," I said with a grin. "Or there would only be one generation of Amazons."

Pam shrugged. "Oh, well, maybe they went off and bopped one on the head when they needed a mate," she said. "But most of the time they were content to be in an all-female society."

"We could always go into a convent and achieve the same thing," I suggested.

She giggled. "Which would you rather put up with: praying on stone floors at two in the morning or worrying about whether Joe Garbarini will ever ask you out?"

"Are you two going to clear off those tables, or do you expect the dishes to find their own way back to the kitchen?" came Joe's grouchy voice through the hatch.

"Stone floors, definitely," I whispered to Pam, and we were both giggling hard as we came through the door with our trays.

On the way home that night, I thought over our conversation. Joe had been grouchy all evening, as if my presence was annoying to him. Pam was right, we'd be far better off without men, I decided. Life would be peaceful, serene, no worries . . . and definitely boring. . . .

I let myself into the condo and the first thing I saw was my mother, curled up on the sofa, staring hard at a public-TV program about molecules.

"As we can see through the electron microscope, the molecules become agitated when . . ." the voice was saying.

Great, I thought. *Even molecules become agitated. It's not even worth coming back as an amoeba!*

"Are you really watching this or have you been asleep?" I asked my mother.

"Really watching," she said. "I've been too angry to sleep. In fact, I've been waiting for you to come home so that I could explode to somebody!"

"What did I do?" I asked, making a mental check of my room, the state I left the kitchen in, the food I'd promised to buy. I couldn't come up with any sin I had committed. The last thing I had done wrong, as far as I could remember, was spoil things between Ralph and her. I still felt pretty bad about that. She was all alone right now, watching molecules on TV, and she could have been out having dinner with Ralph this very moment if it hadn't been for me. Even if I had thought he was a creep, it didn't mean that she couldn't have been happy with him.

I had hoped that constantly being around each other at the *Clarion* would throw them together again, and that he would ask her out once more. But that didn't seem to be happening.

She uncurled and got up off the sofa. "Not you," she said. "That horrible man! Debbie, you were right! I never believed it until now, but you were completely right. Ralph Robertson is definitely a creep."

"What did he do?" I asked, trying to conceal my delight.

"Look at this!" she said, thrusting a newspaper under my nose. I focused on it but couldn't see anything too alarming. Most of the front page was taken up with an article called, "Are We Risking

Our Children's Lives?" which was about hidden asbestos hazards in schools.

"What am I supposed to be looking at?" I asked warily.

"That article!" she said, jabbing her finger onto the page so fiercely that she almost knocked the newspaper out of my hands. "Look at that article."

"It's about asbestos?" I ventured.

"Yes, but who's byline do you see at the top of it?"

" 'By our special correspondent, Ralph Robertson,' " I read.

"And do you know who collected every one of those facts?" she shouted. "I did. It was my article, start to finish. He didn't give me one teeny-weeny bit of credit, the creep! He also had the nerve to thank me for my help in collecting the background data when he'd taken my very words and used them in his article."

"That's too bad," I agreed.

"What's more," she went on, "we had an editorial meeting today. The editor actually complimented him on his hard-hitting material and said he thought it was prizewinning stuff. The creep did not say one word about me. Can you believe it? He didn't even have the grace to say, 'Well, Margaret actually did the research for me.' Even if he didn't want to admit stealing my article, he could have given me credit for helping."

"See, I knew he was a rat," I said. "Must have had a sixth sense about him."

"I'll know next time," she said. She walked over to the fridge and started pouring herself a glass of mineral water. Then she sat on the kitchen stool. "I'm already collecting material for an article on earthquakes," she said between sips. "I'm not going to tell Ralph a thing about that. I'll just hand it straight to the editor when it's ready. I've even learned to save it in the computer under a code!"

"Wow," I said. "Top-secret stuff."

"And you were right about another thing," she went on. "The editor in chief has a new secretary, and Ralph's been hanging around her all week. When I passed them at the water cooler, he was telling her about his crummy fettuccini."

I started to laugh. "See, I saved you from a fate worse than death," I said.

She grinned, too. "On this occasion, I'll have to admit that you did," she said, "but one thing, Debbie . . ."

"Yes?"

"If you ever pull a stunt like that again when I bring a man home, I'll put you up for immediate adoption!"

"Don't worry," I said, "no more childish tantrums, I promise. If you want to bring a guy home, that's fine with me. Maybe we can even go on a double date sometime."

"With whom?" she asked curiously. "I thought you didn't have a special interest in anyone right now."

"I don't," I said. "I just meant for the future—for the day when you meet the right guy and I meet the right guy and we both live happily ever after."

"So the young man with the motorcycle and the hair isn't around anymore?" she asked.

"He's still around," I said. "Minus the hair. His last girlfriend made him cut it, remember."

"Oh, yes, you told me," she said, nodding.

The mere thought of Joe's hair, now neatly tamed from its unruly curls, just peeping out from under his cap as he cooked hamburgers, plunged me back into gloom. I gave a big sigh. "But he just thinks of me as a good and reliable worker. There doesn't seem to be anybody who is interested in me for myself. Grant just wanted me to put the funny parts in speeches, Joe just wants me to clean floors. . . ."

My mother slid down from her stool and came over to me. "Your turn will come," she said. "You're so young. You've still got that magic moment ahead of you when you meet a boy and right away you know that he's the one you've been looking for."

"Like you and Dad, you mean?" I asked.

"Well, I didn't say there would always be happy endings," she said. "At the time I thought your father was the most wonderful thing that could ever happen to anyone. And we did have some wonderful years together. And you, we did have you." She smiled. "I don't think of any of it as wasted time, and I don't want to scare you away from falling in love because of what happened to us. Falling in love for the first time is one of the great experiences of a lifetime, and you've got that to look forward to."

"I hope so," I said. "Pam and I were discussing whether we should become nuns or Amazons or amoebas."

"What?" my mother asked, laughing.

"We've decided love makes life too complicated," I said. "It's not worth the effort."

"But it is," my mother said. "Do you think that someone like me, someone who has been hurt once, would be willing to take the chance again if it wasn't worth it? I can guarantee that each of the happy moments is more than worth every one of the hurts."

"I think I'd be willing to risk the hurts," I said, moving away from her toward the kitchen, "if I could only get past the first hurdle—how to get a guy to ask me out. How to let him know I really like him."

"You could try telling him," my mother said. "Sometimes boys, especially the ones who have a lot of pride, won't risk asking a girl out if they are afraid she might turn them down. Their pride couldn't handle that."

"I see," I said. "Maybe you're right. Maybe I should say something . . . that is, if ever I meet a guy I'd like to date, but who hasn't asked me."

"Of course," my mother said, grinning at me. "If you ever do."

"I'm going to bed now," I said. "To plan what I should say if the occasion ever arises."

"Sweet dreams," my mother called out after me. "And just don't go after anyone who cooks fettuccini. It can lead to nothing but heartbreak."

"There's one or two good things about Heartbreak," I said, and gave her a final smirk before I closed my door.

The next day I drove to the café determined to

settle things once and for all. I had to know whether Joe really liked me or not. I would talk it out with him, or die trying.

Of course, like all good plans, it didn't work the way I planned. I had barely gotten in the door when Joe appeared, taking off his jacket.

"Oh, Debbie, great, you're here. I have to go out for a while. Can you take over right away?" he said.

"Where are you going?" I asked, because I detected urgency in his voice. "Is your grandfather okay?"

"He's here," Joe said. "He's in the kitchen, sitting washing lettuce. He's not supposed to stand, so don't let him. He wants me to get something for him, so you can take over the grill, okay?"

"All right," I said, looking at him suspiciously. I knew Joe pretty well in some ways, and I suspected he wasn't telling me everything. A crazy thought crossed my mind—he was going out to meet Wendy! She had phoned and begged him to meet her again and he was going to. So much for my plans.

Joe was already almost to the front door. "Oh, by the way, there are five orders of burgers and fries waiting to be cooked," he called back to me. "You'd better get going with them in a hurry, and don't let my grandfather help you. He's not supposed to stand up!"

And this was the guy I wanted to tell that I really liked him? I thought angrily. A slave driver who obviously didn't care about me at all. I bet he'd gone to meet Wendy and she'd be back and I'd be looking for another job! Or maybe he'd met another new girl and didn't want to tell me about her. Maybe she'd be ten times worse than Wendy.

Plunged into gloomy thoughts, I put on my uniform in a hurry. I let myself picture the future: a new girl who looked sexier than Miss America, with bright red nails six inches long, sitting on the counter showing her lovely legs and yelling at me to polish the floors, clean the ceilings, wash the windows . . .

"Joe left without cooking those burger orders?" Mr. Garbarini asked, seeing the little order slips still clipped above the grill. "What was he thinking about? Those poor kids have been waiting for hours for their food. You'd better get them out in a hurry or they'll be customers we don't see again."

I slapped five patties onto the grill and went across the kitchen to get five buns. As soon as I moved away, out of the corner of my eye I saw one of the patties start to slide down the grill. I rushed back, but I was too late and it slid down into the sink. This hadn't happened to me since I'd learned to put them on firmly so that they didn't slide when hot fat met cold burger. I went to pick the burger out of the sink, feeling Mr. Garbarini's eyes on me, and had just reached out to it when a second burger started to slide.

"Hey, watch it there," Mr. Garbarini growled. "I don't want to watch all my profits falling onto the floor! Don't you even know how to put burgers on the grill yet?"

"Sure I know," I said. "There's just something funny about this grill today."

"That's right, blame the grill," he said.

"Well, it's nothing I'm doing wrong," I snapped huffily. "I've cooked a million burgers and none of them have slid off."

"Then you'd better turn those other burgers before they burn!" he yelled.

"I can see," I said. "Don't worry. I can handle this kitchen, you know."

I put the spatula under a burger and flipped it. The burger sailed up into the air and disappeared out the open window. I don't know who was more surprised, Mr. Garbarini or me. What was wrong with me? Was I finally cracking up?

"What's the matter with you, eh?" Mr. Garbarini growled, doing a good impersonation of the Godfather and sounding just as terrifying.

"I don't know," I stammered. "That hasn't happened to me since—I just can't understand it." I moved around the grill and peered out of the window over the sink. My burger lay on the concrete and I thought I detected a flash of color as someone disappeared around the corner of the building. Without waiting any longer, I sprinted out of the back door, across the porch, and around the side of the building—smack into Joe, who was standing there pressed against the wall like a little kid playing hide-and-seek.

"I might have known it!" I exploded. I took in the fishing rod in his hand, the transparent line that was obviously attached to my burger. "Of all the dumb, juvenile tricks! I bet you did something to the grill, too, didn't you?"

He nodded. "I oiled it," he said. "Worked pretty

well, didn't it? Your face was wonderful, watching those burgers slide off!"

I glared at him. "May one ask what you hoped to prove? Was it mere juvenile amusement? Were you attempting to make me appear incompetent in front of your grandfather or just to assert your own masculine superiority?"

He grinned. "You're using big words again," he said. "You know I'm just a simple Italian kid."

"Don't give me that stuff!" I shouted. "You know you're just as smart as I am. I know you read books, you like art, and you've got a good brain."

The grin widened. "Can I have that in writing? You think I'm smart and cultured as well as cute?" he asked.

"If your brain was the same size as your ego, you'd have rewritten the theory of relativity," I said, "although I doubt if a simple peasant boy knows what that is!"

"Sure I do," he said, "it's the number of uncles and aunts you can fit around one dinner table. Either that or it's E equals MC squared. Whichever comes first!"

"Sometimes you infuriate me!"

"And sometimes you like me, too," he said. He grabbed my wrists. "Go on, admit it. Sometimes you like to have me around. You like it when I take you in my arms, like this." His arms slid around my waist. "And when I hold you very close, like this. And when I kiss you . . . just . . . like . . . this." And he demonstrated. My arms wrapped around his neck as I melted toward his body.

"Hey, what's going on out there?" Mr. Garbarini's voice rang in our ears. "What you think this is, an adult movie? Eh? If you wanta do that kind of stuff, you do it on your own time, not when I'm paying you, you hear?"

Joe and I broke apart. "You want to do it on our own time?" he asked me, his eyes twinkling. "You want to come down to Uncle Otto's on Friday night and watch the Road Warriors play?"

"Okay," I said. "If there's no trick involved. You're not going to oil the seat there so that I slide down onto the floor, are you? Or rip my dress with a fish hook just to get a laugh?"

He looked at me, tenderly this time. "No tricks," he said, "I promise."

I shook my head. "I don't understand you," I said. "If you like me, too, why do all those dumb things to me?"

He was suddenly serious. "I had to break the spell somehow," he said. "After Wendy came, nothing was the same between us. We never fought anymore, we never teased each other. We were polite to each other. I hated that. I had to do something to get things back to the way they were. I liked our fights, didn't you?"

"Of course I did," I said. "They were the only way I could assert my mental superiority!"

"Ha!" he said. "What mental superiority? Just because you know *War and Peace* by heart does not make you smarter than me."

"And just because you spend a hour a day in front of the mirror doing your hair does not make you sexier than me!" I said back.

"Oh, no?" he asked. "I can get dates by just

snapping my fingers. I whistle and they come running."

"Oh, yeah," I asked. "What do you have, a dog whistle?"

"You heard the call," he said smugly. "And don't deny it!"

"Did I ever mention that you were very annoying sometimes?"

"Every day," he said. "But don't change. I like you the way you are. I don't want a relationship like the one with Wendy. I want us to be the way we've always been, okay?"

"Fine with me," I said.

"Great," he said, beaming at me. "Now get inside, woman. I bet you've burned those hamburgers by now!"

I attempted to grab him. He dodged aside and I found myself tangled up in fishing wire. "Joe Garbarini, I'll get even with you if it's the last thing I do!" I yelled after him as he ran back inside the café.

Here's a look at what's ahead in Catch of the Day, *the fourth book in Fawcett's Heartbreak Cafe series for GIRLS ONLY.*

We were all astounded when Art walked into the Heartbreak wearing red shorts, a white T-shirt, a red visor, and had a whistle around his neck.

"This has to be quick," he said, sliding into the nearest seat. "I'm on my way to work," he added and looked at us with a big, triumphant grin.

"I don't believe it," Joe called through the hatch. "The biggest surf-rat on the beach got a job? Someone was really dumb enough to hire you?"

"You are looking," Art said dramatically, "at a full-fledged Rockley Beach lifeguard."

"A lifeguard? You?" Joe called back.

"Why not?" he asked. "I'm a strong swimmer, and I know beaches and oceans better than anyone."

"But don't you have to be qualified—you know, take some kind of test?" I asked.

"I took them, this week," he said. "They were real short of guards, so they had this intensive course. I passed everything, of course. I swam better than anyone there."

He looked round and beamed at us again. "So, how's this for a cool job?" he demanded. "I get to sit on the beach, sip a cool drink from time to time, talk to cute girls in small bikinis . . . and get paid for it!" He burst out laughing. "Man, this has to be the wildest joke—getting paid for hanging out on the beach, which is what I do anyway."

"I think they expect you to do more than sip drinks and talk to girls," Joe cautioned.

"Yeah, you might actually have to save someone," I reminded him.

"So? I'll need to get wet from time to time, you know. Give me an excuse to run into the ocean."

He got down from his seat and straightened his visor. "Come on down and visit me," he said. "You can watch me in action, soaking up the rays for six bucks an hour!"

"I don't believe it," Joe muttered as we all watched Art head toward the beach.

"You have to admit, that guy always lands on his feet," Art's buddy Josh complained admiringly. "I'd always thought about lifeguarding, but I heard you had to go to school for weeks. Not our Art. He gets the crash course and is qualified in a few days!"

"Yeah, luck is not the word for Art," Joe added. "I bet he sold his soul to the devil when he was a little kid."

"We'll have to go down and check him out," Josh said with a laugh.

Later that day Joe and I went to the beach to see Art at work. He was sitting, just as we'd imagined, on his tall lifeguard's chair. His long legs were stretched out in front of him and he was leaning down to one side, a soda can in his hand, talking to an admiring group of girls.

"Tough life," Joe muttered to me.

"I don't think his supervisor will be too pleased if he comes around and sees Art goofing off like that," I whispered to Joe.

"Who says he's goofing off?"

"He's talking to those girls."

"But he's also watching the ocean," Joe said loyally. "Which is what he's paid to do."

Just then I heard a shrill laughter coming from down the beach where a group of girls were standing at the edge of the ocean, squealing as they jumped over each wave. I caught Art's eye and he grinned.

"Nice legs," he commented, then he glanced down the beach. "You guys better go," he said. "Looks like the boss is coming this way, and I'm not supposed to talk to friends when I'm on duty."

As we walked away I noticed a wave that was bigger than the rest, the sort of freak wave that high winds out at sea sometimes churn up. I heard yells and saw a mother rush to pick up a kid playing with a bucket. The girls we noticed earlier saw it too—except for one of them, who was standing, still laughing and jumping, with her back to the ocean. The huge wave struck her in the middle of her back and swept her off her feet as she disappeared under the foaming water.

In seconds, Art leapt down from the chair and sprinted down the few yards of beach, grabbing the lifeline as he ran toward the beating surf. The water was still so turbulent that it was impossible to catch more than a glimpse of the girl. I hadn't seen her face at all, just a flailing arm or foot now and then, as if a rag doll were being tumbled around. Art strode powerfully into the surf, reached down, and came up with the spluttering, struggling girl in his arms, then carried her back efficiently to the shore.

In the midst of a general murmur of congratulation, Art stood with a big grin on his face. "Hey, you know what?" he called to me, catching my eye through the crowd of admirers. "Being a hero could be fun!"

JANET QUIN-HARKIN lives with her family near the beach in northern California, but she says the true inspiration for HEARTBREAK CAFE was the years she spent on the Australian beach in search of sunshine and surfers. More than five million copies of Ms. Quin-Harkin's books have been sold around the world, including the hit series SUGAR & SPICE. Ms. Quin-Harkin and her husband have three daughters who attend the University of California and a son in high school.

Eat Your Heart Out
in the
HEARTBREAK
CAFE

FOR GIRLS ONLY

by: Janet Quin Harkin

ideals®
MOTHER'S DAY

Long years you've kept the door ajar
To greet me, coming from afar:
Long years in my accustomed place
I've read my welcome in your face....
—ROBERT BRIDGES

IDEALS PUBLICATIONS

NASHVILLE, TENNESSEE

Home to Mother
Author Unknown

No matter how far our feet may rove,
When weary and worn in constant strife,
Mother and home are the best of life.

Blessed is he who may smilingly say,
"I'm going home to mother today."
God's mercy hallows that home so dear,
Where Mother our footsteps waits to hear.

Bless the busy hand and the cheery smile
That brighten and comfort all the while;
Nothing on earth can with home compare
When a loving mother waits us there.

Mother
Author Unknown

As long ago we carried to your knees
The tales and treasures of eventful days—
Knowing no deed too humble for your praise,
Nor any gift too trivial to please—
So still we bring with older smiles and tears,
What gifts we may to claim the old, dear right:
Your faith beyond the silence and the night,
Your love still close and watching through the years.

Photograph by Marion Brenner/Botanica/Jupiter Images

Mother's Day Greetings

Pamela Kennedy

The racks are full of Mother's Day cards once more. Browsing through them, I find verses penned in bold calligraphy and dainty script, some with softly faded photographs and others with eye-catching graphics. There are so many choices; one could find just about any type of card for any type of mother. There are few cards, however, that will ever be as treasured as those children write in their own trembling hands in the years when they have learned to communicate through the written word, but are still innocent enough to be totally honest about how they feel. I know, because I have a collection of these cards garnered from the childhoods of my three children. Whenever I feel a bit down about my mothering, I bring the cards out and read them once again.

Probably the first Mother's Day card every modern-day mother receives is the one Sunday school and preschool teachers create each year. I have received variations on this card from each of my children. The card sports a hand-print, or sometimes two, on a plain construction paper background. (I am still in awe of any teacher who allows a classroom of youngsters to run around with paint-covered hands.) Inside the folded paper is a copy of the following poem:

Sometimes you get discouraged
Because I am so small
And always leave my fingerprints
On furniture and wall.
But every day I'm growing up
And soon I'll be so tall
That all those little fingerprints
Will be hard to recall.
So here's a final hand print
So someday you can say,
"This is how your fingers looked
For Mother's Day in May."

I have no idea who wrote this little verse, but I know for sure that her kids were young. The reason I know is that fingerprints don't go away; they just move higher up the wall and eventually may even be found on the ceilings! The verse is a nice sentiment and something a first-time mother should receive at least once in her life.

After graduating from the handprint and mimeographed poem stage, the time comes for the best Mother's Day cards—the time when the children actually compose their own verses. In kindergarten and first grade, the mere fact that spelling is not refined makes for some interesting greetings. My son once gave me a card addressed

Photograph by Steve Terrill

to the "the beast Mom in the hole world!"

My daughter had a problem with writing letters backward and turned her p's around to wish me a "Very Haggy Mother's Day! I would like to attribute their original greetings to mere immaturity and not to some Freudian slip.

During second and third grade, my children began to try their hands at poetry, and the verses they created on Mother's Day are the ones I read when I need to take myself a little less seriously. My son's third grade teacher compiled a leaflet of poetry containing an entry from each child in the class to his or her mother. The poems all followed the same pattern: the word Mother was followed by two adjectives, then a phrase or two describing something they admired about her, then closed with a synonym for Mother. I read through about twenty of these little gems and smiled at how tender and sweet they were. Then I came to my son's. My nine-year-old realist had penned:

> Mother
> Loving, Caring
> Helps me with my homework,
> On a scale of 1–10, I give you a 7, Mom.

I was not sure if that was a compliment or a complaint, but I expect he felt I had some room for improvement!

My daughter, Anne, prefers rhyming verse and came up with the following for her Mother's Day offering:

> My Mother is very, very neat.
> She is the person you'd like to meet.
> She knows what love means.
> She's always pretty clean.
> There's nothing quite like a mother.
> Not a sister or father or even a brother.

Anne is obviously not given to flowery words, nor is she prone to exaggeration—at least not in the case of my virtues! But there are certainly worse things to be remembered for than cleanliness.

My children are now a bit older and more sophisticated, and they have abdicated the role of greeting card writer to professionals. They thoughtfully choose sentiments properly aligned on bond paper and written in the smooth meter of the accomplished poet, but I still cherish the broadly traced script painstakingly scrawled on notebook paper. In the poetry of my children's cards, I find my affirmation as a mother. These are the people who live with me day in and day out, who know all my failings and still rate me as neat, clean, and a perfectly acceptable seven!

Soft and gentle—
Soft and gentle as the petals of the rose
Are my Mother's hands.
In childhood she stooped
And clasped my face
With her dear loving hands.
And smiled away my tears.

—ANNA MIKESELL BYERS

Mother's Day
Edgar A. Guest

Let every day be Mother's Day!
Make roses grow along her way
And beauty everywhere.
Oh, never let her eyes be wet
With tears of sorrow or regret,
And never cease to care!
Come, grown-up children, and rejoice
That you can hear your mother's voice!

A day for her! For you she gave
Long years of love and service brave;
For you her youth was spent.
There was no weight of hurt or care
Too heavy for her strength to bear;
She followed where you went;
Her courage and her love sublime
You could depend on all the time.

Let every day be Mother's Day!
With love and roses strew her way,
And smiles of joy and pride!
Come, grown-up children, to the knee
Where long ago you used to be
And never turn aside;
Oh, never let her eyes grow wet
With tears, because her babes forget.

THE ROSE GARDEN by Edmund Blair Leighton.
Image from Fine Art Photographic Library, London

Bouquets of Love
Joy Belle Burgess

When the meadowland was gleaming
With tints of green and gold,
I would frolic in the grasses
And the flowers' magic fold,

To fill my arms with sunshine
Where the dandelions grew,
That I might bring my treasures
Of lovely spring to you.

And when the sun was shining
Its warmth upon the hill,
I would sit amongst the buttercups,
Delighted in the thrill

Of their wild and gay profusion
Of petals yellow-gold,
And I would pick for you, dear Mother,
All my eager arms could hold.

I could not wait to bring you
The fairest spring bouquets,
Bright blossoms that would wish you
A happy Mother's Day.

For the flowers on the hillside
Beneath the skies above
Were the richest gifts that I could give—
My sweet bouquets of love!

Photograph by Dennis Frates

The Sweet Smell of Sunshine

Faith Andrews Bedford

ood morning," I say as I hear my sister's step on the stair. "Did the smell of the biscuits wake you?"

Ellen smiles. "No, I've been up for a bit. But speaking of aromas, what do you wash your sheets in? They have such a wonderful scent."

"That's the smell of sunshine."

Ellen looks puzzled. "A new detergent?" she asks. "I haven't heard of that one."

"No," I laugh and point to my clothesline, strung between two trees in the backyard. "I hang my laundry out on that line. The combination of the fresh breezes and sun dries them in no time."

I press a linen tea towel to my face and breathe deeply. "And I love the way it smells."

"I'd forgotten clotheslines," Ellen says with a smile. "Remember when we used to help Grandy hang out the clothes?"

Our grandmother hung her laundry out on a line strung between her house and the barn. The line hung in a neat coil on the side of the barn for most of the week; but on Mondays, she would pull it out taut and fasten it to a large metal hook on her house. If we were around on washday, she would dub us "Mistresses of the Pins" and tie her clothespin aprons—yellow calico with red rick-rack on the pockets—around our waists.

From a distance, our rhythm must have looked like a lovely *pas de deux*: Grandy bending gracefully down to the wicker basket, pulling out a piece of laundry, giving it a sharp snap to straighten it out, and placing it over the line; Ellen and I reaching up to hand her the clothespins.

When I had children of my own, I loved hanging the tiny baby clothes and diapers on the line and gathering them a few hours later, sweet-smelling and fresh. Something about sunshine seemed to keep the girls' batiste baby dresses sparkling white. And the diapers were so easy to fold, dried smooth as they were by the wind.

Sometimes the clothesline provided live theater for the children.

"Look, Mommy," they would giggle as they gazed out the window. "The clothes are dancing." Sitting on the window seat, we would watch together as my husband's jeans did high-kicks and my nighties swayed back and forth, waving their arms in graceful arcs.

The clothes on the line often serve as a sort of barometer, warning me of an impending storm. As a low-pressure system moves in, the clothes hang limply from their pins. Then, as the storm approaches, they begin to flap, not with the regular, undulating wave of a steady, drying breeze, but with a nervous twitching. When they begin to whip about wildly, I race out to gather them before the rain hits. Often, I get the laundry into the basket in the nick of time, and big drops pelt me as I streak for the house.

Sometimes, I am too late. Distracted by some other chore or deeply engrossed in writing, I do not realize a storm is upon me until I hear the first clap of thunder.

"The laundry!" I'll gasp as I run to the door, only to be stopped by a curtain of rain. I slump against the window, watching the rain sluice from the sky, drenching the clothes. There they hang, poor things, water pouring into pants' pockets, rain running in rivulets down the shirts.

But there's something about clothes that have had a final rinse of rain. When the sun breaks through and they are dry for a second time, they have a special fragrance—sort of spicy and sweet combined.

Occasionally, I will forget to bring the laundry in at night. If the moon is full, the clothes look like phantoms blowing and moving eerily in the moonlit air.

"Look," I would say to the children. "There are ghosts in the backyard."

"Ghosts?" they would shout and run to the windows.

"Oh, Mom," they would groan in unison when they beheld my so-called spirits. I was only able to pull that off two or three times.

The children used my clothesline too. When two sheets were pinned up, they made a perfect curtain for the Bedford Family Players. Although it may not have been a heavy sweep of red velvet, many a young actress or actor has made an entrance from behind that improvised curtain. Several appreciative audiences have gathered on blankets or in lawn chairs to watch a neighborhood production of *Swan Lake* or *Little Red Riding Hood*.

The clothesline became an integral part of the children's outdoor "let's pretend." If I lowered the line a bit, we could drape an old double-bed sheet over it, secure the corners with stones, and, voilà—a tent! The children would fill it with pillows and dolls, tea sets and dress-ups; and, pretty soon, they were camping in the wilderness on their way west to discover gold in the California mountains, the tent keeping them safe from (teddy) bears.

"Don't you have a dryer?" Ellen asks as we take our breakfast tea outside to enjoy the warm sunshine.

"I do," I answer. "But I really prefer my solar-powered one. Hanging the clothes on the line saves electricity, and I don't have to iron as much."

Ellen nods and then adds, "The clothes do smell wonderful."

I smile in agreement and then think of another benefit. "Besides," I laugh, "all that bending down to the basket and reaching up to the line has got to be good for my waist."

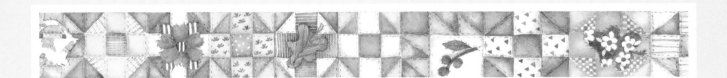

*My brothers were collectors of anything curious,
from the odd to the mundane: bottlecaps, marbles,
gum wrappers, rubberbands, store string.
Mom always found their booty whenever she
did the laundry. There she found stuffed into
pockets the history of the day.*

—PATRICIA O'BRIEN PARKER

The Clothesline

Helen Gregory

I caught a glimpse of Mama
Hanging out the clothes;
I still recall that fragrance,
As sweet as any rose.

The simple little dresses
That Mama made for me
Were washed and dried, hung outside,
Between the clothesline trees.

I still can feel the gentle wind
Brush against my cheek;
And when the clothes were neatly hung,
The sun played hide-and-seek.

Blowing here, billowing there,
At last the clothes were dried;
'Twas no place I would rather be
Than with the clothes outside!

WOMAN PUTTING WASH ON THE LINE *by Camille Pissarro.*
Image © SuperStock, Inc./SuperStock.

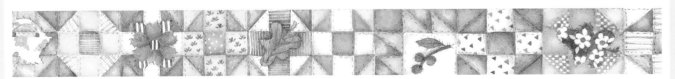

The Threads That Bind

Kerrie Flanagan

After enduring a few stitches and a couple of minor surgeries, it was a relief when the most recent operation was successful. My seven-year-old son, Drew, was thrilled. These were always rough times for him, but the older he got, the easier they became. With this last attempt, a few more months, maybe even a year, were added to the life of his favorite blanket.

With a look of sadness and concern in his blue eyes, he had approached me one morning holding his blanket like it was a wounded animal. His blond hair stood in all directions, obviously the result of a rough night's sleep.

"Mom," his voice cracked. "There are more holes. Can you fix them?" I looked at the wounded piece of fabric in his hands. I gently picked it up by the corners to assess the damage. Big holes and frayed edges. Careful not to pull on any of the life-bearing threads, I said to him, "I'll see what I can do, honey."

Like a skilled surgeon, I carefully examined the patient. This was not going to be easy, but I came up with a plan. I called Drew over for my prognosis. "Your blanket isn't looking so good. If it's okay with you, I will sew it to some other fabric and patch up the holes. Okay?"

He agreed and then reluctantly put his priceless possession into my hands before we left for school. I felt I should have had him sign a medical release form before he left, freeing me from all responsibility should something go wrong. (I am not the best at sewing; truth is, I am not very good at all.)

After an hour of skillful work (luck, actually), the surgery was a success. My reward—a big smile showing both of his adorable dimples, a hug and a "Thank you, Mommy," that oozed with sincerity.

Some people may say Drew is getting too old for a blanket, and I should just throw it away. Part of me agrees with that, but then another part remembers wrapping him up in that same blanket and rocking him to sleep. This blanket has been more than just a source of comfort at night; it has been a superhero cape, a bandage for wounded stuffed animals, a spread for a picnic, and a memory keeper for me. I miss holding him in my lap, his head resting on my chest, the powdery fragrance of a freshly cleaned baby.

I could tell him he is too old for a blanket

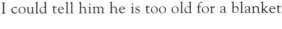

SPOOLS *by Rebecca Barker.*
Copyright © 2002 by Rebecca Barker

and that it is time for him to grow up, but why? If you think about it, adults have favorite "blankets," too: an old night shirt full of holes or a car stranded in the garage we swear we are going to fix some day. We would never admit we have favorite "blankets," things in our lives that provide us comfort and that we'd have a hard time doing without.

So what will I do when Drew needs me to fix his blanket again? I'm not sure. For now, I kiss him good night, tuck his blanket snugly to his chin, and tell him to have happy dreams. I slip into my favorite holey nightshirt, grab my favorite quilt and a family photo album, and nestle into my favorite chair. With a big sigh, I open the album and begin reliving moments of the past seven years—many with a little boy and his favorite blanket.

Family Recipes

Ladyfingers

2   tablespoons butter
¾   cup plus 2 tablespoons all-purpose
      flour, sifted
4   egg yolks
½   cup granulated sugar

4   egg whites, beaten until stiff
      Pinch of salt
1   teaspoon vanilla extract
      Confectioners' sugar for dusting

Preheat oven to 350°F. Grease and flour 2 baking sheets with 2 tablespoons butter and 2 tablespoons flour. Set aside.

In a large bowl, combine egg yolks and granulated sugar. With an electric mixer fitted with a wire whisk, beat on medium-high speed about 8 minutes until the mixture is thick and pale yellow and has tripled in volume. Fold in beaten egg whites, remaining ¾ cup flour, salt, and vanilla.

Stir gently until mixture is smooth. Transfer batter to a large pastry bag with a ¾-inch plain tip. Pipe fingers about 4 inches in length, about 1 inch apart, onto the baking sheet, using the lines as a guide. Dust the ladyfingers with confectioners' sugar. Bake 15 to 18 minutes, or until just firm on the outside and soft in the center. Makes 24 ladyfingers.

Ginger Tea

1   1-inch piece ginger root, peeled
1   large strip lemon rind
6   cups water

⅓   cup honey
      Juice of one lemon
4   chamomile or other tea bags

Slice the ginger into coins. Heat the ginger, lemon rind, water, and honey to a boil in small pot. Add lemon juice to hot water and transfer to a tea pot. Add tea bags to pot and steep. Remove bags and serve. Makes 4 to 6 servings.

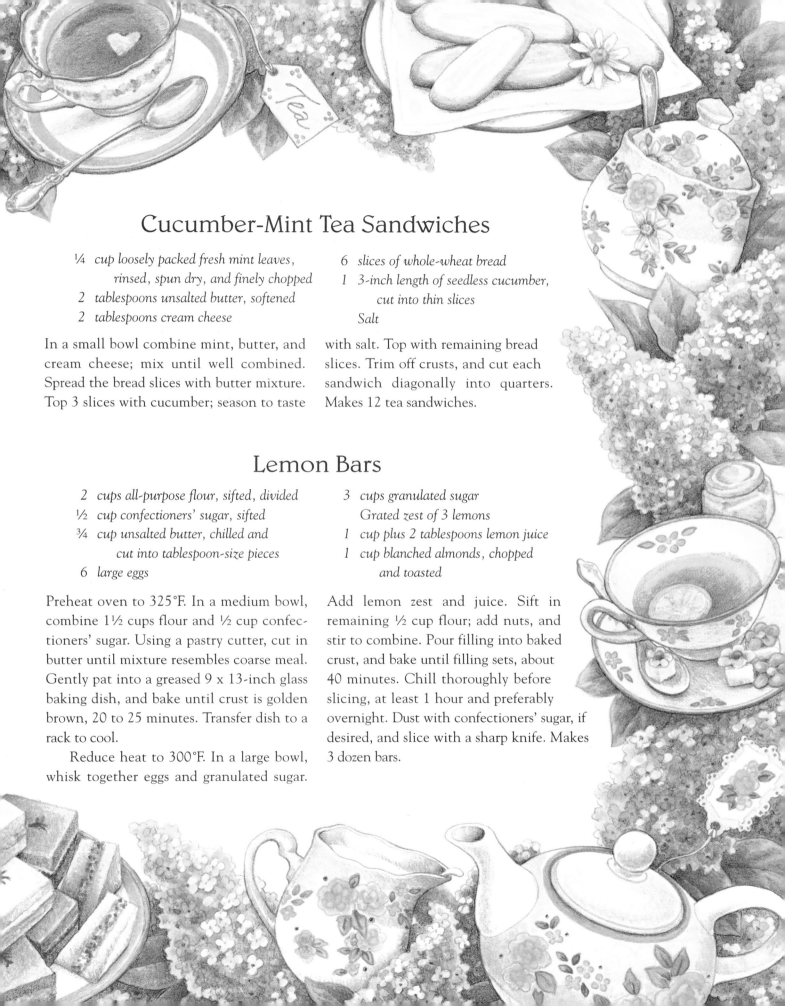

Cucumber-Mint Tea Sandwiches

¼ cup loosely packed fresh mint leaves,
       rinsed, spun dry, and finely chopped
2 tablespoons unsalted butter, softened
2 tablespoons cream cheese

6 slices of whole-wheat bread
1 3-inch length of seedless cucumber,
       cut into thin slices
   Salt

In a small bowl combine mint, butter, and cream cheese; mix until well combined. Spread the bread slices with butter mixture. Top 3 slices with cucumber; season to taste with salt. Top with remaining bread slices. Trim off crusts, and cut each sandwich diagonally into quarters. Makes 12 tea sandwiches.

Lemon Bars

2 cups all-purpose flour, sifted, divided
½ cup confectioners' sugar, sifted
¾ cup unsalted butter, chilled and
       cut into tablespoon-size pieces
6 large eggs

3 cups granulated sugar
   Grated zest of 3 lemons
1 cup plus 2 tablespoons lemon juice
1 cup blanched almonds, chopped
       and toasted

Preheat oven to 325°F. In a medium bowl, combine 1½ cups flour and ½ cup confectioners' sugar. Using a pastry cutter, cut in butter until mixture resembles coarse meal. Gently pat into a greased 9 x 13-inch glass baking dish, and bake until crust is golden brown, 20 to 25 minutes. Transfer dish to a rack to cool.

Reduce heat to 300°F. In a large bowl, whisk together eggs and granulated sugar. Add lemon zest and juice. Sift in remaining ½ cup flour; add nuts, and stir to combine. Pour filling into baked crust, and bake until filling sets, about 40 minutes. Chill thoroughly before slicing, at least 1 hour and preferably overnight. Dust with confectioners' sugar, if desired, and slice with a sharp knife. Makes 3 dozen bars.

Mother's Tea Set
Anne Norman

Around these entwined and faded
Roses, the jam pots, the smell
Of baking, the lidless sugar bowl,
And the amber-stained pot,
You opened your woman's world
To me: how good friends
Are as necessary as air;
How to hold my chin up and push
The world away with one
Deep breath; how to knead
Biscuit dough only ten times,
More makes them tough; and
That men need strong women
And strong coffee. Layer by layer,
Cup by cup, my role, your life,
Was revealed.

Your chipped cups still hold
The sweetness of my world.

Find yourself a cup of tea;
the teapot is behind you.
Now tell me about hundreds of things.

—SAKI

Photograph by Alison Gootee/Botanica/Jupiter Images

Side by Side
Sherri Waas Shunfenthal

Side by side
With my daughter
Making a cake from scratch

Flour
Butter
Water
Eggs

Sugar to add sweetness
To our day
We stir and stir

Memories
Myself as a little girl
Baking joyfully with my mother
Side by side

Cookie Time
Lee Simmons

In retrospect I well recall
My mother's baking day
With pies and cakes and crusty bread
In fragrant, neat array.

For those were special, magic hours . . .
How does a mother know?
When she would let me pat and cut
A bit of cookie dough.

That mound of dough, once
    creamy white,
Would soon be laced with grime,
As one small cook, dissatisfied,
Reshaped time after time.

And when at last each piece
    was baked,
My day was quite complete,
For happiness was surely there . . .
Right on a cookie sheet.

And now my daughter has a home
And children of her own,
And someday she will share
    with them
The happy things she's known.

And as her memories rush back,
It would be nice to know
That she, like I, still cherishes
The joy of cookie dough.

Photograph by Jessie Walker

Like Mother Used to Make

Marjorie Holmes

The other day, I read in a readers'-request column this plea: "Can someone please tell me how to make old-fashioned apple strudel? I have the recipe my mother used, but somehow my apple strudel never turns out the way hers did, and I'm wondering what I could be doing wrong."

Will she ever find the secret? I, too, wondered. No matter how many readers try to help her, how many suggestions she receives about the extra dash of sugar, the freshness of the butter, the temperature of the oven, the timing of the baking, will anyone ever be able to reproduce the magic formula that was her mother's and hers alone?

Like Mother used to make . . . Bakers long have claimed the slogan; advertisers have lured us with it to their pickles and catsups and jellies and jams.

Like Mother used to make . . . The very words conjure up a kitchen where a woman toils lovingly to fashion her family's favorite dishes. It paints a nostalgic picture of children flocking around wanting to help—to beat the eggs, to stir the batter, to roll out the piecrust, to cut the cookies, to handle the bread dough. It re-creates a hundred small, significant scenes—of people who come sniffing into a kitchen, begging a taste of this, a nibble of that, peering into the oven and pleading, "Something smells good. Is supper ready? I'm starved."

Like Mother used to make . . . The cheese soufflé. The nut bread. The chicken casserole. The potato pancakes. The cherry pie. The Christmas plum pudding.

Recipes we have aplenty, passed along to daughters, presented to sons' brides. "Johnny is awfully fond of upside-down cake. I always made it this way." And eagerly the young wife follows directions, does her best to duplicate that special dish. But she knows, even when he's too polite to tell her, that something is different about it. Whatever her skills or practice, something is missing, some rare, lost ingredient that not even the best-intentioned cook can supply.

Because a mother stirs a little bit of herself into everything she cooks for her family. Unseen, all unsuspected, into the bowl goes the subtle flavor of her personality—the way she thinks and feels, the way she laughs or tilts her head or scolds. And into this dish of hers, too, go the whole measure and taste of the home—the way the dining room used to look when the lamps were lighted, the sound of family voices, the laughter, the quarrels, the memories.

These are the ingredients we lack when we try to reproduce the dish that Mother used to make. These are her secret spices. They are not for sale, and they can't be passed along.

Yet every woman who enters a kitchen carries with her a rare and precious store of her own. The flavor of herself in relation to her children, the warmth and tang and savor of her own household. Daily, inescapably, without ever realizing it, all of us are blending these inimitable components into other dishes, into other lives.

So that one day our children, too, will say, "My mother used to make the most wonderful peach cobbler. I can't make it come out the same, no matter how hard I try!"

Photograph by Jessie Walker

Through the Eyes of Her Child

Kathryn Byron

Her outstretched hand
was silken and smooth,
yet rough and tired,
from holding up our house.
She called to me
with a familiar voice;
such a calm and soothing tone.
Her scent was
as native as flowers.
It was sweet-smelling and fragrant,
yet not stored in any bottle or spray.
She would lock me up in her arms.
Her violet sweater
was old, worn, and faded,
but still soft against my cheek.
No matter how hot or cold
it was outside,
she was always
the right temperature.

My mom is a never-ending song in my heart of comfort, happiness, and being. I may sometimes forget the words, but I always remember the tune.

—GRAYCIE HARMON

Photograph by Jessie Walker

A Tribute
Mildred Maralyn Mercer

All that I can give to life will be
To hold a crimson sunset in the sky,
Or catch a birdsong as it flutters by
Or string the stars on moonbeams that I see . . .
And for the rest who often wonder why
You do so much, and how your hands can fly,
Will be an unforgotten melody.
My poems and songs can only be the leaves . . .
Your life has been the tree.

Mother
Louise D. Ross

Now that I, too, have heard from baby lips
The name of "Mother," I can truly know
The splendor of your life, your griefs, your pain.
Closer than kin, we three,
Boughs of one parent tree.
In my own babe, you see your child again;
In me, yourself. And in your aging face,
I glimpse myself in prospect. May the grace
And beauty of your life descend to me.

Photograph by Dennis Frates

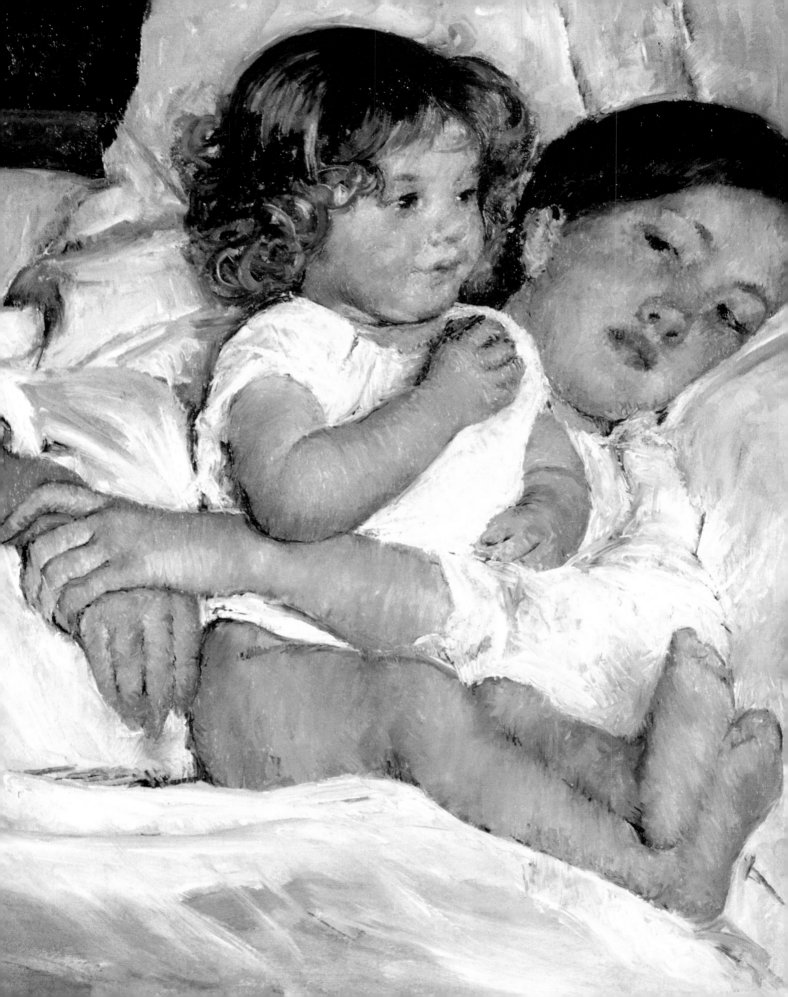

In the Circle of Your Arms
Deborah A. Bennett

If ever there was sadness,
They drove away my tears.
If ever there were words to share
Or nothing left to say,

If ever I was angry
And no one understood,
If ever I should worry, they'd be
There to see me through.

If ever I should long to share
Some simple moment's joy,
Or ever I was lonely for a
Voice to echo mine;

If ever I have doubted
That I was truly loved,
Every fear I had has vanished
In the circle of your arms.

Human Affection
Stevie Smith

Mother, I love you so.
Said the child, I love you more
than I know.
She laid her head on her
mother's arm,
And the love between them
kept them warm.

The Second Motherhood
St. Clair Adams

A child was born to me today,
A birth without a throe;
Joy thrills within me, but the pain
Died thirty years ago;
For 'tis the child of him I bore,
And well may he entwine
His dearest hopes about it; still,
'Tis mine, and ever mine.

And I shall comfort all its hurts,
And weep when it is ill,
And know some portion of the grief
A mother knows; but still
The care, the watchful discipline
Through all the years must fall
To other hands—for me such things
Have passed, and love is all.

The child I bore, himself made good
All my distress and pain;
And now the child that comes to me
From heaven is pure gain—
And his child will be mine. And his.
I'll down the ages go
In glad, perpetual motherhood
Through births without a throe.

Photograph by William H. Johnson

The Christening Gown

Faith Andrews Bedford

Several months ago our son, Drew, called. "Hi Mom," he said. "You're going to be a grandmother again."

Although I had been anticipating the news for some time, I was not prepared for the tears that suddenly filled my eyes. As I hung up the phone and told my husband the news, he grabbed me and we danced around the kitchen whooping with laughter. When we caught our breath, Bob said, "Looks like the christening gown will be worn again."

I nodded and looked back a few years to when our first grandchild, Carter Elisabeth, was born. The first thing I did when I learned of her impending arrival was to find the family christening gown. I had not seen it in nearly twenty-five years.

As I climbed the stairs to the attic I remembered how carefully I had packed the gown away after the christening of our last baby. I had wondered then how many years would pass before I would get it out again.

I found the box lying in a dim corner. Carefully untying the ribbons that fastened the lid, I unfolded the tissue paper and caressed the soft, creamy folds of silk.

The gown is so old that its once-sparkling whiteness has softened to a pale ivory. The narrow hand-sewn seams are carefully rolled so no rough stitching will ever touch a baby's soft skin. Delicate handmade lace edges the little collar and the sleeves, and rows of little tucks have accommodated babies both large and small. The gown has been worn both by tiny newborns and strapping one-year-olds; it has been taken in and let out many times.

Six generations of Bedfords have worn this gown and its matching silk coat and bonnet. The initials of each child and their birth date have been carefully embroidered in the lining—some more skillfully than others.

"I don't know how to embroider!" I confessed to my grandmother as my own firstborn's christening day approached.

"Here, dear, I'll show you," she patiently replied as she set me to practicing on a bit of white muslin. The thread broke, knots formed, letters straggled.

"Won't you please do it?" I begged.

She simply shook her head. "It's a mother's privilege," she said.

I finally felt up to the task and carefully embroidered *W.A.B. 8-2-1964.* Grandmother was very proud of me.

As I lifted the dress and looked at my handiwork, I was proud, too. With each child I'd grown more proficient. Drew's initials had been done in tiny cross-stitch; Eleanor's were in block; Sarah's flowed in graceful curlicues. I ran my fingers up the long row of initials and dates until I reached the first set: *N.P.B. 1-4-1863.*

In the bottom of the box is a little pouch into which have been slipped photographs of almost all of the babies who have worn this dress. . . . Our own children's christenings marked new chapters in our marriage, for each one was born in a different city. The happy memories of every new home are captured in the photographs of our babies' christenings.

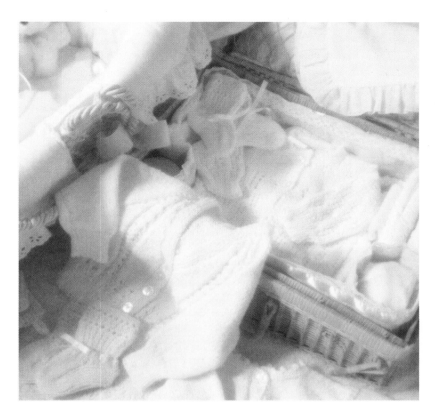

The christening gown has traveled with each generation, first by flatboat, later by horse and wagon, then by steamship, automobile, and truck. For Carter it made its first trip by plane. The previous wearers had all been Eastern babies, but for Carter's christening, the little dress traveled to the mountains of Utah.

I carefully mended a seam and checked the stitching on the tiny pearl buttons, then I folded it gently back into its box. Smoothing the soft silk in place was like touching a butterfly's wing. It is delicate but enduring. Despite more than a century of christenings, the precious heirloom looked as though it could be worn for a century more.

As I walked to the village to mail the gown, I pondered my new role. For thirty years I had worn many hats: wife and mother, teacher and volunteer, farmer and writer. I realized that I would soon have a brand-new hat to wear—a grandmother's hat.

Carter had not even arrived yet but already I felt venerable, as though a mantle of wisdom had been gently placed upon my shoulders.

At the post office I met an old friend, Guy, who had been a grandfather for at least a dozen years. As we stood in line, I told him the good news of the soon-to-be birth of our first grandchild. I confessed to being a bit nervous in this new role and asked him what being a grandparent truly means. "A grandparent," he told me solemnly, "is someone who tells the stories."

"Well then, here, Jan," I said as I pushed my package across the counter to our postal clerk. "Send this off to Drew and Jill. It will be the first chapter of the old stories."

Soon the christening gown will be worn again by the latest addition to the newest generation. Sitting on the porch, sipping tea, Bob and I wonder out loud how many more times it will be worn by our grandchildren. Where else will it travel? Will we live to see it worn by our great-grandchildren?

I smile. The answers to those questions will be part of the new stories. I look forward to telling them.

Featured Poet

To a New Mother

Eileen Spinelli

Last night was
sweet and uncertain,
long with tears
and tumbling lullabies.
Still sleepy,
you tiptoe across
a tangle of toys.
Don't wake the baby.

Come
sit for a moment
while the rooms are quiet.
Sip tea from the blue mug.
See how the sunlight
dances across the grass.
Look how the flowering tree
blooms wild and pink
and how the robin sings
near the window . . .

for you

for you.

Happy Mother's Day.

The New Mother

Margaret J. Seibold

A different place, a different year,

A newborn child, so sweet, so dear.

I counted the fingers, I counted the toes,

And kissed the little turned-up nose.

This child, so perfect in every way,

Had joined our life on this wonderful day.

So this Mother's Day tribute I've written to you

And this newborn, nestled at your breast, so new.

And you too will also

Count the fingers and pink little toes,

And kiss the little turned-up nose,

And whisper, "I love you," as she sleeps
      in your arms,

And take in all of her wonderful charms.

A different place, a different year,

We welcome this baby, so sweet, so dear!

*A mother's arms are made
of tenderness, and children
sleep soundly in them.*
—VICTOR HUGO

Photograph by Jessie Walker

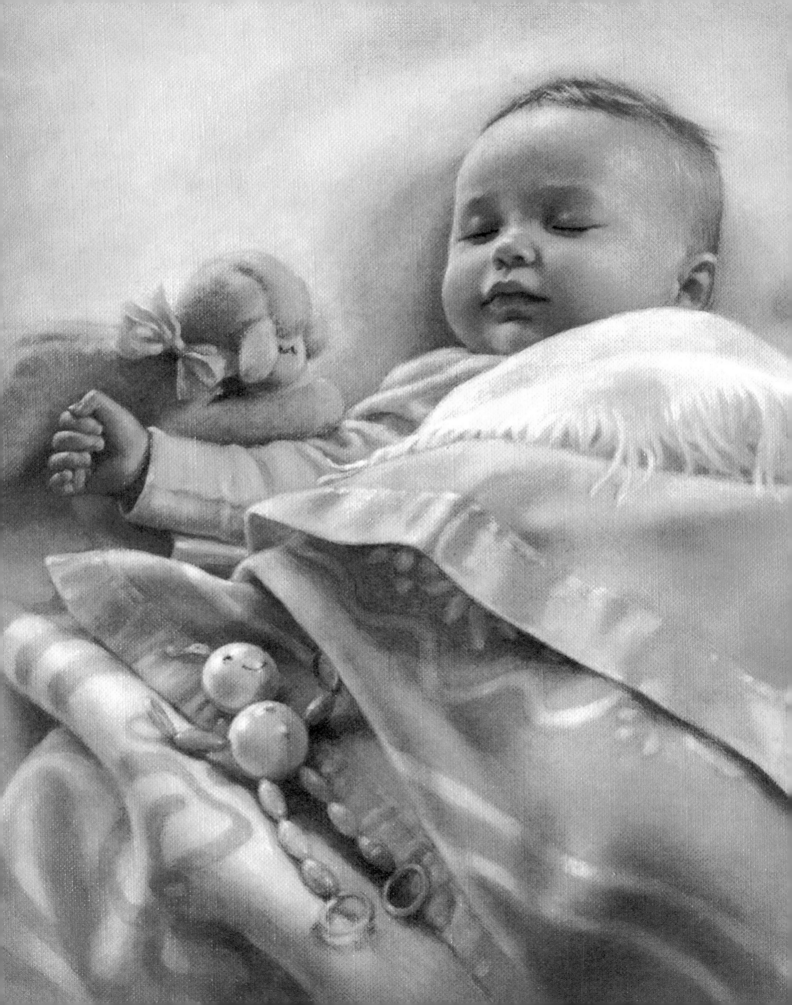

Mother

Henry Chappell

There's a hand so firm and tender
As it holds the cords of home
And guides each wayward footstep,
That heedless yearns to roam;
That smoothes the roughest places
And stills the childish fears;
Is ever there to help the play
Or dry the rainbow-tears.

There's a voice that makes the darkness
Of the little bedroom light;
All the bogies fly its music
And the nasty dreams take fright,
As it tells of shining angels
Who watch the whole night long,
Till the sun peeps thro' the lattice
And the lark begins his song.

There's a heart so true and steadfast,
That, save the One above,
No tongue can tell its pity,
No words describe its love.

Bits & Pieces

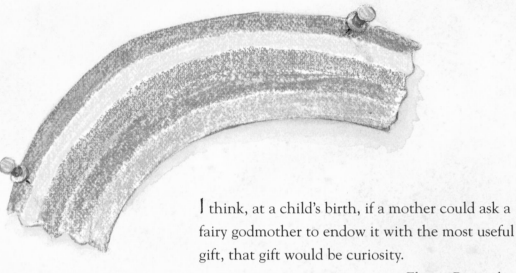

All children are artists. The problem is how to remain an artist once he grows up.
—*Pablo Picasso*

I think, at a child's birth, if a mother could ask a fairy godmother to endow it with the most useful gift, that gift would be curiosity.

—*Eleanor Roosevelt*

A mother's example sketches the outline of her child's character.
—*Mrs. H. O. Ward*

No painter's brush, nor poet's pen
In justice to her fame
Has ever reached half high enough
To write a mother's name.
—*Author Unknown*

Mama exhorted her children at every opportunity to "jump at de sun." We might not land on the sun, but at least we would get off the ground.
—*Zora Neale Hurston*

The mother's heart is the child's schoolroom.
—*Henry Ward Beecher*

Carousel

Veronica Hosking

The world would definitely be a brighter place if we could only capture the magic found in a carousel ride and share it with everyone. Remember what it felt like when you went to the amusement park and heard the carousel music playing?

Your palms itched to feel the reins in their grasp, and your heart beat faster in anticipation of the adventure. Was there ever a little girl or boy who could resist its whimsical melody? Everyone wanted a chance to ride their horse off into a world of their own creation. Little girls pretended to be princesses, and little boys pretended to be brave knights.

Until I took my daughter on her first carousel ride, I had forgotten what hold this simple ride could have on a person.

It did take a bit of coaxing to get her on the first time, and even then she wouldn't go up on a horse. But once the carousel started turning and its music began playing, the magic took over; and a wide-eyed, three-year-old girl looked around in fascination.

"Mommy, why are the horses going up and down?" she asked with eyes glued on the horses in front of us.

I laughed and pulled her closer to me. "It's supposed to feel like you're riding a real horse."

She stared in awe at the horses. "Oh," she sighed in love. "Can I try one?"

"Of course you can," I replied with a smile.

When the ride stopped, we turned around and got back in line for another go. The second time was even better than the first. This time she sat up on a horse with reins in hand and laughed through the whole ride.

Now, she pretends to be on a carousel wherever we go.

One day while we were playing in the neighborhood park, she came running up to me with a huge smile on her face. "Mommy! Mommy! I want to ride the carousel," she pleaded, pulling me onto the grass.

"Rachael, there isn't a carousel here to ride," I explained as I tried to figure out where she was leading me.

Rachael pointed in the direction we were going and said, "It's over there, Mommy." She stopped in front of a tree and said, "See, it's a blue horse. Can I ride it?"

Most of the trees in our park have a base trunk and then fork off into two separate trunks, making a V pattern that is easy for a child to straddle. After Rachael pointed out the horse to me, I realized this was what she wanted to do. I stood there in total bewilderment as to how her little mind saw this tree as a horse.

Rachael tugged on my shirt again. "Put me on, Mommy. Put me on!" I picked her up and she straddled the tree trunk and held on to the part that was in front of her. "You have to start the ride, Mommy."

"Okay, sweetie. It's started," I replied.

"No it isn't. The controls are over there." She pointed to a storm-sewer cover.

I shook my head and then walked over and stood on the cover of the storm sewer. "Here?" I asked with raised eyebrows.

"Yes!" She kicked her horse. "Turn it on."

I grinned and pretended to push a button in the thin air in front of me. "There, it's on," I said, shaking my head in disbelief.

"Yay!" she squealed in amusement. Then she began patting her horse's mane. "I have the prettiest blue horse on the carousel, Mommy."

I was still standing on the storm-sewer cover, envious of my daughter's vivid imagination. I smiled and said, "Yes, you do, sweetheart."

After a little while, Rachael looked at me and said, "Okay, the ride's done."

"Okay," I said. I proceeded to help her out of the tree.

"No, Mommy! You have to turn it off!"

Silly Mommy—she forgot we were on a carousel! I stepped back on the storm sewer cover and pressed another pretend button.

Rachael smiled wide and patted her horse again. "You were a good horse. Thank you for the ride."

I leaned over and helped Rachael out of the tree, and she ran over to another tree and said, "I want to ride the gray horse now."

For the rest of the afternoon, Rachael ran from tree to tree and announced which color horse she wanted to ride. She was crestfallen if she came to a tree that forked off too high for me to get her in the saddle.

I carried my exhausted little girl home, knowing the magic of a carousel ride would inspire her for a long time to come. As we crossed our front porch into our house, Rachael lifted her head off of my shoulder and offered me a weary smile.

"That was the best carousel ride I never had, Mommy." Then she laid her head back down on my shoulder and closed her eyes.

I smiled and brushed my hand over her hair. I couldn't see the horses she rode so enthusiastically all afternoon. The heart-racing imagination of a child is spectacular to witness firsthand.

Gifts
Sheila O'Connor

Of all the small things we are given to love—
new grass, acorns, the mystery of seeds,
February's warm breath, raspberries,
    lilacs in the spring—
I love you most of all
because you have given them back to me.
A keen eye for the moon,
gentle fingers tracing a sidewalk's crack,
the lacy web of a fly's wing.
You have taught me to taste the world again,
swallow dry snow,
smell the surprise of the January sun.
You, my small scientist of beauty,
recover the wonder of life
in your open, astonished hands.

What Matter?

Marjorie Ross Garver

She let the vacuum cleaner whir
To listen to a sweeter sound,
That of the ceaseless hummingbird,
Dipping into the flower faces.
And if she let the dinner burn,
What matter? She had tales to tell
Of the squirrel's cheeks puffed out,
Hoarding nuts in a hollow tree.
And what if toys were sometimes scattered?
There were always flowers on the table,
Valley lilies pearled with rain.
If mud were tramped in by careless feet,
What matter? She could tell long stories
Of puppies splashing through spring puddles,
And of triumphant harmonies born
Of wind's dances in the treetops.

Photograph by Jessie Walker

Mother-love, God's gift to His children,
With heavenly fragrance fraught;
The brightest flower in God's garden,
His truest forget-me-not.

—MYRTIE FISHER SEAVERNS

Mother's Garden
Author Unknown

A fresh little bud in my garden,
With petals close folded from view,
Brightly nods me a cheery "good morning,"
Through the drops of a fresh bath of dew.

I must patiently wait its unfolding,
Though I long its full beauty to see;
Leave soft breezes and warm, tender sunshine
To perform the sweet office for me.

I may shield my fair baby blossom;
With trellis its weakness uphold;
With nourishment wisely sustain it
And cherish its pure heart of gold.

Then in good time, which is God's time,
Developed by sunshine and shower,
Some morning I'll find in the garden
Where my bud was, a beautiful flower.

Photograph by Aflo/relax/Jupiter Images

Grandmother's Garden

Gail L. Roberson

I used to keep my lawn and gardens spit shined. There was a place for everything, and everything was in its place. Thank goodness I survived those days. Now I have the garden my grandma had that I first fell in love with as a child and that set me for life with the desire and green thumb for gardening.

Today my garden is more relaxed and enjoyable, and it has become an interesting transformation of beds and borders of both blowzy-wild and planted bouquets and aromatic herbs. From the earlier days, when I rushed out to find seeds sprouting and tiny plants taking root, I've added an azalea here and there, a hydrangea or two, a spot of chives, a dash of rosemary, some self-sustaining succulents, rose of Sharon shrubs, evergreens, and tossed everywhere handfuls of seed pods left from Grandma's high-stalk, pink-headed phlox—just to name a few items in my garden surrounding my studio.

As a girl, I used to hide in Grandma's flowerbeds. Some of them were so tall and thick with old-timey blossoms that I could easily disappear altogether, especially in her hollyhocks. Her beds reached out in the air to capture stray seeds of things we never could identify, and they rambled off in the direction of a nearby hedgerow with only room enough to slip the push mower through between them. I absolutely loved it. I'd search for something new in them every day.

She had hardy, stemmed blossoms to arrange on the church communion table late each Saturday afternoon, and constantly jam down into the big cut glass vase, romantic and bright. Now and then, a tomato seed that had escaped from her garden would be staked right where it sprouted alongside the peonies at the front of the house. Even in the vegetable garden, she maintained a row of colorful marigolds, zinnias, and asters for her vases. There was always a row of spearlike, stately gladiolus staked against the wind for cutting all summer.

Grandma's garden and I grew together. When I was a child, her gardenias were pinned to my Easter dresses; I put them in my hair during my teens, and in vases in my home later, rooted directly from hers. I remember the smell of her garden dirt. She mixed ashes from her wood heater along with soil from the chicken yard, and it grew grand things.

Of course, Grandma was already along in years when I was a child. She didn't sweat the small stuff that the weather and the seasons brought to her gardens, but just loved them for what they were at the time. Hers. Done her way. At her pace.

I have also now learned to cultivate Grandma's viewpoint, allowing my garden to grow according to its own pleasures. I snatch a weed now and then and take pruners in hand when I feel like it. Otherwise my garden goes the way of Grandma's. Like her, I finally acquired the wisdom of going native. Today my garden is a diamond in the rough where there remains little area to even spread the mulch. It is filled with surprises at every turn. Little things I never saw before bring great merriment to my soul. Weeds have some of the prettiest blossoms of all when left alone long enough to do so. I wouldn't have thought so, long ago. But gardening brings wisdom.

Photograph by Steve Terrill

Generational Gardening

Wilma Cooper

When I was growing up, my mother made me help her with weeding the flower beds. Certainly I had no interest in learning that chore. Once I even chopped down her bed of day-lillies. However, when I was married and we moved from one location to another, I could hardly wait to start the landscaping. I insisted that my daughters help; and they vowed that when they had their own homes, they would never garden.

Now, each of them has beautiful and unique gardens—flowers, vegetables, and herbs—and each of them is her own gardener. I'm waiting with great interest to see if the green thumb has been passed along to Mama's great-granddaughters.

Photograph by Nancy Matthews

Small Offerings
Kim Konopka

In my overgrown garden, I weed,
trying to untangle a season of neglect.
Across the yard, from an old hose,
my daughter collects water into
cupped hands and slowly
walks the offering toward me.
The liquid dribbles between soft
fingers, sprinkles small bare feet.

She arrives, arms stretched high
then sees she has nothing to give me.
My gloved finger points to her toes
glistening with the last drops
and tears begin to form.
Leaning down, I bring her hands
to my lips and swallow all
her empty drink and whisper,

Pretend water is so much sweeter.

Grandmother Hens

Susan B. Townsend

It has been almost twenty-two years since I became a mother and took the first hesitant steps of the most amazing journey of my life. I'd be a fool to dispute the passage of time, but part of me is astonished—and, I confess, a bit frightened—that so many years could slip by with so little effort. Like a tiny pebble tossed in the lake, the time has disappeared with barely a ripple.

While countless people have come and gone in my children's lives, my place in their hearts has remained secure. Someday soon, however, our dance together will end, and when the next song begins, they will be facing new partners—the ones they've chosen for the rest of their lives.

Like the other changes I've experienced as a mother, this one will have its bittersweet moments, but I'm confident that the smiles will far outnumber the tears. I welcome the opportunity to share my children's joy and their sorrow, if need be, as they start their own lives. I am delighted by the thought of our family growing to include their spouses. And I love the idea of becoming a grandmother. Grandchildren are like the paycheck you receive after working countless hours of overtime at the best job you've ever had.

Twenty-two years ago, I wondered if I would be a good mother, and because babies don't come with instructions, I suffered through many moments of anxiety and plain old panic. Those early months of my son's life were rife with crises, and I still have the stack of dog-eared books I consulted for every burp and every sniffle. It was my own mother, however, who gave me what I really needed.

Looking back, I realize it wasn't her words that made the difference. It was her silence. Her advice was readily available and eagerly shared—but only when I asked for it. By standing back and allowing me to find my own way, she gave me the chance to develop the self-confidence that would carry me through the challenges she knew were coming. She taught me to trust my instincts, and by raising me with unconditional love, she gave me the greatest gift of all. I'm not worried about whether or not I'll be a good grandmother. If I continue to rely on the legacy of life lessons my mother left behind, I have a feeling I'll do just fine.

Early last fall, I noticed that one of my young hens was sitting on her first clutch of eggs. I've always been impressed with the dedication of a hen determined to hatch out a brood of chicks, and this pullet was no exception. She rarely left her nest, and when she did, it was only to take in life-sustaining food and water.

One day, while I was feeding the chickens, I noticed her amongst the group scratching and eating at my feet. When I looked across the pen to her nest, I was surprised to see one of my older hens sitting on the eggs. Later, when I looked again, the pullet had resumed her position on the nest. The old hen remained close by, but it was obvious she had no intention of interfering with the younger bird. I was charmed by the thought that the older chicken was like a grandmother, standing by in case she was needed and stepping in when the pullet needed a break.

Grandmothers come in all shapes and sizes. Some have gray hair and wear pearls, while others have burgundy streaks and wear a nose ring. Some knit and others skydive. There are grandmothers who bake cookies and ones who burn toast. Despite the differences, they all have one thing in common: the opportunity to make a difference in their grandchildren's lives. I hope I make the most of that opportunity. I pray that I will have what it takes to stand back and let my children find their own way, to teach them to trust their instincts, and to leave a legacy of love that endures long after I'm gone.

I Should Be So Lucky
Jane Butkin Wagner

I see my daughter looking
at us, side by side, as if we're two pieces
of her jigsaw puzzle.
She looks for sameness; she searches for
identifiable differences.

Finally
She tells me:

> Mom! You have your mama's voice.
> Mom! You have your mama's hands.
> Mom! You have your mama's smile.

She laughs:

> Mom! You're turning into your mama!

I laugh back:

> I should be so lucky.

When I stopped seeing my
mother with the eyes of a child,
I saw the woman who helped me
give birth to myself.
— NANCY FRIDAY

The precursor of the mirror is
the mother's face.
— D. W. WINNICOTT

MOTHER COMBING HER CHILD'S HAIR *by Mary Stevenson Cassatt.*
Image © Brooklyn Museum of Art, New York/
Bequest of Mary T. Cockcroft/The Bridgeman Art Library

To My First Love, My Mother
Christina G. Rossetti

Sonnets are full of love, and this my tome
Has many sonnets: so here now shall be
One sonnet more, a love sonnet, from me
To her whose heart is my heart's quiet home;
To my first love, my mother, on whose knee
I learnt love-lore that is not troublesome;
Whose service is my special dignity,
And she my lodestar while I go and come.
And so because you love me, and because
I love you, Mother, I have woven a wreath
Of rhymes wherewith to crown your honored name:
In you not fourscore years can dim the flame
Of love, whose blessed glow transcends the laws
Of time and change and mortal life and death.

My Mother
Beulah Windle Scallin

All shining crowns do not adorn the brows of kings;
Nor scepters rule by might alone. As precious wings
Are often cased in chrysalis of slender mold
And jewels reckon more of worth than weight in gold,
My little mother measured greater than she knew;
In spirit boundless as the ether-vaulted blue,
Her quiet mission the sustained embodiment
Of beauty's strength. Her inmost being—confident
Of truth and justice in the cosmic plan—was strong
To live a message of exalted love and song;
To face impending hardship with undaunted mind;
And through a full life's usefulness, keep sweet . . . be kind.

West Dennis, Massachusetts. Photograph by William H. Johnson

Mother's Heart
Linda C. Grazulis

I've heard the power of thunder
And felt the pitter-patter of rain,
Watched a rainbow arch in splendor
As a breeze rustled a meadow's lane.
Oh, to see a tiny rosebud
With grace unfold and bow,

And to hear the sweet laughter
Of a contented, happy child!
Yet in all the blesings bestowed on me
None can quite impart
The warmth, love, and tenderness I feel
Coming from my mother's heart.

My Mother
Florence R. Andrews

So gracious, and so sweet,
Such willing hands and feet,
There's nothing quite complete
Without her.

The love light in her eyes—
Her tender words and wise
Make earth a paradise
About her.

We bring all to her side,
Newborn, and happy bride;
Loved counselor and guide—
My mother.

Photograph by Jeremy Samuelson/Botanica/Jupiter Images

Most of all the other beautiful things in life come by twos and threes, by dozens and hundreds. Plenty of roses, stars, sunsets, rainbows, brothers and sisters, aunts and cousins, but only one mother in the whole world.

—KATE DOUGLAS WIGGIN

ISBN-13: 978-0-8249-1318-2

Published by Ideals Publications, a Guideposts Company
535 Metroplex Drive, Suite 250, Nashville, Tennessee 37211
www.idealsbooks.com

Publisher, Peggy Schaefer
Editor, Melinda Rathjen
Copy Editor, Kaye Dacus
Designer, Marisa Jackson
Permissions Editor, Patsy Jay

Cover: Photograph by Stromburg/Premium Stock/Jupiter Images
Inside front cover: Painting by George Hinke. Image from Ideals Publications
Inside back cover: Painting by George Hinke. Image from Ideals Publications
Additional Art Credits: "Bits & Pieces" art by Jodi Wheeler; "Family Recipes" art by Kathy Rusynyk; *Spools* by Rebecca Barker, courtesy of Rebecca Barker's Quiltscapes (www.barkerquiltscapes.com); *Cherished Memories* by Greg Olsen, courtesy of Greg Olsen Art, LLC, 1-208-888-2585 (www.gregolsenart.com); *Sweet Dreams* by Kathy Lawrence, from the Visions of Faith Collection, courtesy of Mill Pond Press Companies (www.millpond.com).

ACKNOWLEDGMENTS:

BEDFORD, FAITH ANDREWS. "The Sweet Smell of Sunshine" and "The Christening Gown." Previously published in *Country Living*. Reprinted by permission of the author. COOPER, WILMA. "Generational Gardening" from *Mothers & Daughters Forever*, edited by Karol Cooper, published by Walnut Grove Press. Used by permission of Caroline Ross. FLANAGAN, KERRIE L. "The Threads that Bind" from *Chicken Soup for the Mother and Son Soul*, edited by Jack Canfield, published by Health Communications, Inc. Used by permission of the author. GUEST, EDGAR A. "Mother's Day" from *The Book of Mother Verse*, edited by Joseph Morris. Used by permission of the author's Estate. HOLMES, MARJORIE. "Like Mother Used To Make." Previously appeared in *McCalls* magazine. Used by permission of Dystel and Goderich Literary Management. HOSKING, VERONICA. "Carousel." Copyright © 2002 by Veronica Hosking. From *Forget Me Knots…From the Front Porch*, compiled by Helen Kay Polaski, published by Obadiah Press. Used by permission of the author. SMITH, STEVIE. "Human Affection" from *Collected Poems of Stevie Smith*. Copyright © 1972 by Stevie Smith. Reprinted by permission of New Directions Publishing Corp. TOWNSEND, SUSAN B. "Grandmother Hens" originally "Closing Thoughts About Grandmothers" from *A Bouquet for Grandmother*. Copyright © 2007 F&W Publications, Inc. Used by permission of Adams Media, an F&W Publications, Inc. company. Our Thanks to June Cotner, editor of *Mothers and Daughters*, published 2001, by Harmony Books, Random House, for her excellent book and her assistance in locating the following authors: KATHRYN BYRON for "Through the Eyes of Her Child," KIM KONOPKA for "Small Offerings," SHEILA O'CONNOR for "Gifts," JANE BUTKIN ROTH for "I Should Be So Lucky," and SHERRI WAAS SHUNFENTHAL for "Side by Side." Our thanks to the following authors or their heirs: St. Clair Adams, Florence R. Andrews, Deborah A. Bennett, Joy Belle Burgess, Anna Mikesell Byers, Marjorie Ross Garver, Linda C. Grazulis, Helen F. Gregory, Pamela Kennedy, Mildred Maralyn Mercer, Anne Norman, Patricia O'Brien Parker, Gail L. Roberson, Louise D. Ross, Beulah Windle Scallin, Margaret J. Seibold, Leeta Simmons, Eileen Spinelli. Every effort has been made to establish ownership and use of each selection in this book. If contacted, the publisher will be pleased to rectify any inadvertent errors or omissions in subsequent editions.